City Murders

Spear Books

1. *Sugar Daddy's Lover* Rosemarie Owino
2. *Lover in the Sky* Sam Kahiga
3. *A Girl Cannot Go on Laughing All the Time* Magaga Alot
4. *The Love Root* Mwangi Ruheni
5. *Mystery Smugglers* Mwangi Ruheni
6. *The Ivory Merchant* Mwangi Gicheru
7. *A Brief Assignment* Ayub Ndii
8. *Colour of Carnations* Ayub Ndii
9. *A Taste of Business* Aubrey Kalitera
10. *No Strings Attached* Yusuf K Dawood
11. *Queen of Gems* Laban Erapu
12. *A Prisoner's Letter* Aubrey Kalitera
13. *A Woman Reborn* Koigi wa Wamwere
14. *The Bhang Syndicate* Frank Saisi
15. *My Life in Crime* John Kiriamiti
16. *Son of Fate* John Kiriamiti
17. *The Sinister Trophy* John Kiriamiti
18. *My Life in Prison* John Kiriamiti
19. *My Life with a Criminal: Milly's Story* John Kiriamiti
20. *Black Gold of Chepkube* Wamugunda Geteria
21. *Nice People* Wamugunda Geteria
22. *Ben Kamba 009 in Operation DXT* David Maillu
23. *The Ayah* David Maillu
24. *Son of Woman* Charles Mangua
25. *A Tail in the Mouth* Charles Mangua
26. *Son of Woman in Mombasa* Charles Mangua
27. *Kenyatta's Jiggers* Charles Mangua
28. *A Worm in the Head* Charles K Githae
29. *Comrade Inmate* Charles K Githae
30. *Twilight Woman* Thomas Akare
31. *Life and Times of a Bank Robber* John Kiggia Kimani
32. *Prison is not a Holiday Camp* John Kiggia Kimani
33. *The Operator* Chris Mwangi
34. *Three Days on the Cross* Wahome Mutahi
35. *Birds of Kamiti* Benjamin Bundeh
36. *Times Beyond* Omondi Mak'Oloo
37. *Lady in Chains* Genga-Idowu
38. *Mayor in Prison* Karuga Wandai
39. *Confession of an AIDS Victim* Carolyne Adalla
40. *The American Standard* Sam DeSanto
41. *From Home Guard to Mau Mau* Elisha Mbabu
42. *The Girl was Mine* David Karanja
43. *Links of a Chain* Monica Genya
44. *The Wrong Kind of Girl* Monica Genya
45. *The Other Side of Love* Monica Genya
46. *Unmarried Wife* Sitwala Imenda
47. *Dar es Salaam By Night* Ben Mtobwa
48. *A Place of No Return* Mervill Powell
49. *The Verdict of Death* Onduko bw'Atebe
50. *The Spurt of Flames* Okelo Nyandong
51. *The Unbroken Spirit* Wanjiru Waithaka
52. *Tower of Terror* Macharia Magu
53. *The Nest of my Heart* Florence Mbaya
54. *City Murders* Ndũcũ wa Ngũgĩ

City Murders

Ndũcũ wa Ngũgĩ

SPEAR
BOOKS

Nairobi • Kampala • Dar es salaam • Kigali

Published by
East African Educational Publishers Ltd.
Elgeyo Marakwet Close, off Elgeyo Marakwet Road,
Kilimani, Nairobi
P.O. Box 45314, Nairobi - 00100, KENYA
Tel: +254 20 2324760
Mobile: +254 722 205661 / 722 207216 / 733 677716 / 734 652012
Email: eaep@eastafricanpublishers.com
Website: www.eastafricanpublishers.com

East African Educational Publishers also has offices or is represented in the following countries:
Uganda, Tanzania, Rwanda, Malawi, Zambia, Botswana and South Sudan.

*This book is dedicated to the memory of
my mother, Nyambura wa Ngũgĩ, and that of
my brother-in-law, George Waithaka.*

ISBN 978-9966-25-981-3

ACKNOWLEDGEMENTS

I have a lot of people to thank for making this book come to life. James, Trish, Khalif and Amira Atwater for their support during the creative process; Jimmi Makotsi for initial edits; Professor Laban Erapu for a superb job of editing the final draft; Henry Chakava and Jane Mathenge for staying the course with me; and my publisher, East African Educational Publishers. I would be remiss if I did not mention Dr. Emilie Paille from whose class assignment at Mercer College the idea of the story was spawned. A special thanks to my father, Ngũgĩ wa Thiong'o, for your tireless critiques of the many drafts of this book; to Maitũ Njeri wa Ngũgĩ for your encouragement; to my brothers and sisters - Tee, Kĩmunya, Mũkoma, Ngina, Wanjikũ, Njoki, Bjorn, Mũmbi and TK for the juicy stories, some of which might have shaped characters in the book; to Mĩring'ũ for your sense of humour, To my nieces and nephews, the N's (Nyambura 1 and 2), Biko, Chris, June, EJ, Geneva and Gabrielle for allowing me to dream; to my sister-in-law, Anne Kamau, for your insights on the book; a very heartfelt and warm thanks to my wife, Grace Gathũngũ, for your love and support during those long days and nights of writing and re-writing. Lastly, to my daughter, Nyambura wa Ndũcũ - you are the best.

Much love.
Ndũcũ wa Ngũgĩ
Long Island, NY, USA 2014

Chapter One

●━●━●━·━●━●━●

A small crowd gathered around the newspaper stand by my bus stop talking excitedly about an event – a death, or something. I stood at the far end smoking a cigarette, trying to mind my own damn business. From the tidbits drifting my way I gathered that it must be someone important – but I could not have cared less. I was not in a curious mood. I had woken up late, with a hangover that could have effortlessly felled a few men and I was headed to work!

The bus ride did not help matters much. The conductor, a young man wearing an oversized T-shirt with *Atlanta Braves* printed in the front, gave me wrong change from a large bill that I had just handed to him. In fact, it was the only such bill he was holding, folded between his middle and index fingers so that it stuck out like flaps on a paper plane. I was not about to let him get away with it – money was already so tight!

"You gave me the wrong amount," I said, holding out my hand to show him the change he had handed to me.

He looked at me for a while and then turned around, ignoring me. I am not a small man by any standard but my youthful looks belie my actual size. Or he must have thought I was a pushover, given my huddled posture between two other passengers.

"Give me back my change right now!" I raised my voice, summoning that feeling which my friend Otieno called "the animal."

I felt a gnawing anger, a fury, that had once propelled me to knockout a well-built wanna-be gangster who had confronted me outside Broadways Tavern a few years back.

"I gave you the correct change!" he said and gave me a long stare, all the while chewing loudly on his bubble gum.

"Who the hell do you think you are fucking with?" I asked him, trying to squeeze myself up from my seat. One of the passengers, sitting to my right, spoke up and told the conductor that they had seen me give him the bill. Reluctantly, the conductor handed over the rest of my change with a few choice words that I did not care for.

At work, the secretary informed me that the boss wanted to see me. We had nicknamed him Bulldog, more from his bullish ways than by the broad shoulders he carried on a small frame. What now? I wondered as I steadied myself to meet with him.

"Jack Chidi reporting for duty, sir!" I croaked, a little phlegm catching in my throat. I would normally stand at attention with a fake salute – that of a private in the presence of a superior officer - but that morning, I did not have the energy.

It was something I had done for too long to quit now but one that started out as a joke. We had accidentally found out that Bulldog had had a stint in the army, just after college, but was discharged when he accidentally shot himself in the foot. He had long stopped seeing the humour in the act but it was one of those things, even in its oddity, that had become part of the office culture.

I pulled up a chair and sat down. He pushed a copy of the morning paper towards me.

"Have you seen this?" he asked, not looking up but continuing to stare at his computer screen.

"*KING'ORI IS DEAD!*" the headlines read in bold.

So was this what they were talking about at the bus stop? An old black and white file-photo of him smiling accompanied the story. He looked younger than his age and more energetic but there was something else about his smile that seemed out of sorts. It was, perhaps, a reminder that he had had better days at some point in the not-too-distant past.

"I want you to cover it," Bulldog whispered. "Find out all you can." He was still staring at his computer screen the way a concerned parent does at an ailing child. I did not see what the big deal was. King'ori was just another dead Kenyan. As I waited for further instructions from Bulldog, I stared at his balding head on which little beads of perspiration had begun to form.

His office still exuded that familiar musty smell of old papers piled up carelessly, competing for space on the floor around him and on the bookshelves behind his desk. I looked around, wondering how he ever managed to find anything amidst that clutter.

Bulldog had good connections to top government officials and members of the business community with whom he spent an inordinate amount of time, hobnobbing at get-togethers, official functions and dinner parties. He enjoyed it when they came to him for favourable coverage, but he was not one to shy away from reporting any shenanigans that these same people engaged in. To say he was always fair and balanced would be fallacious but he took his work seriously and did not bow to pressure by powers that be.

He stopped caressing the keyboard for an instant to look at me, perhaps wondering why I was still there.

"Is that all?" I asked more out of awkwardness than necessity.

He turned his lower lip as if to sneer at me but he did not say anything for a minute.

"I'm not sure what you will find but we need a good follow up - anything you can dig up," he said and turned back to his computer. So that was it! Bulldog was a man of few words.

I stood up slowly and walked out of his office, heading to my desk. My head was still throbbing. I tried rubbing my temples to relieve the pressure that threatened to burst it open. I hated that I had drunk too much last night and the headache was enough to remind me that it was time to slow down.

Needing something to perk me up quickly, I walked to the lounge at the end of the office building, grabbed a Styrofoam cup from the cabinet and poured myself some coffee from the dispenser. I added two teaspoonfuls of brown sugar and idly watched the crystals disappear in the black brew. Just then Otieno, my colleague at work and a friend, came in. He poured himself a cup too and sat down on the dilapidated couch that served as a bed on those rare occasions when one needed to pull an all-nighter.

"How are you doing this morning, Jack?" he asked after taking a noisy sip of his coffee.

I sat down next to him. I did not feel like talking but I needed to fill in some gaps from the night before. What a night! I remembered that Mburu, my cousin, and Ali Fana, our detective friend, had joined us for a drink after work but I could not string the events that followed clearly.

"How did we get home?" I asked.

"Dude, you were on fire," Otieno said, grinning widely as if re-living the highlights.

At five foot five and on the lean side, Otieno had one of the widest grins I had ever seen on anyone. It was his constant companion even when performing the minutest of tasks but it suited him well.

"Oh man, don't tell me I made a fool of myself again," I said.

"Mburu and Ali left just before midnight but you insisted that we stay on and sample a few more bars," Otieno said amidst sinister sounding laughter. "I think we must have gone to all the haunts in Uthiru before we finally caught a taxi home. I did not know you could move like that!" He sipped on his coffee. His bloodshot eyes darted swiftly my way but he did not meet my tired gaze.

"And what were you doing while I was carrying on?" I asked, digging a little.

I remembered sitting somewhere with a group of women, singing an off-tune rendition of *Malaika*. I had a vague recollection of Otieno huddled in a corner with some woman, a brightly lit jukebox standing in a corner and what seemed to be a plethora of JVC speakers surrounding a makeshift dance floor complete with a stroboscope.

"It was a good night," he said dismissively as he stood up and walked back to his desk.

I needed to start working on my new assignment. I passed by Otieno's desk, fighting back the urge to seek more answers about the previous night. He was already on the phone with someone and when he saw me, he covered the mouthpiece with his hand and turned to face me, expectantly. I waved him to carry on, signaling that I would be back later.

At my desk I continued sipping on my coffee absent-mindedly. I perused the morning paper, gazing at the black and white photos of President Joakim, taken the previous day at a fundraiser for a secondary school in Kajiado District.

We were the only paper that used black and white photos, which according to Bulldog, gave us an originality that was not coloured by modernity. He had smiled at his play of words but I knew it was this kind of thinking that had us struggle to compete with other newspapers and online journals. The only thing that saved us was our fearless and hard-hitting coverage of stories.

I flipped the paper back to the front page. King'ori, with that infectious smile, was still staring right at me, his eyes imploring. I turned the page and came to a photo montage of King'ori, with family, standing in front of an electronics store and the most recent one with him sitting on a dais. He was at some fundraiser with the president and now, he was dead. Was there a connection? I wondered, as I began to read his story.

King'ori was born in Njoro to farming parents who scraped day in and day out to provide for their son. Despite his humble beginnings, he rose through the ranks at Takana Electronics, starting as a lowly shop assistant and ending up as outright owner. His vast wealth had raised his social stock and he was often seen in the company of the top political leadership. President Joakim called him "my friend" and often sought his counsel.

It was possible that this friendship had cost him his life, I thought. But why was I assuming it was an assassination? Nothing in the report gave any indication of how he died. Was it murder, suicide or did he succumb to a protracted battle with some illness? It did not make a difference - the man was dead.

I sat back on my chair and closed my eyes. Where would I begin? As an investigative journalist, my task was to dig deeper and get behind the news reports but it always helped when there were glaring misrepresentations of facts, financial scandals, suspicious deals or illegal contracts. I enjoyed chasing the paper or money trails, piecing together the missing links to expose stories that would have otherwise remained secret lives. Here I was, chasing death!

The investigative process was the same. I started posing questions and scribbling little notes for my own reference. Who was King'ori? How did he die? Who would want him dead?

I grabbed my phone to call detective Ali to get more details but I quickly put it back on its cradle. I did not know what to ask him; it always helped to have some form of preparation before calling someone to get information. One could lose a lead on a story by posing the wrong questions, even to a friend - and in this business you could not afford to mess up by going in unprepared or insufficiently prepared. It made you look like an amateur. Or - like Otieno liked to say - it was like running in the dark with your eyes closed.

I opened up the paper again but the pounding in my head was unbearable. The letters jumped around with every throb. I set it aside for a minute. I had to deal with this god-forsaken hangover somehow. I should have called in sick and slept all, damn, day long.

I folded the paper, put it in my coat pocket and walked out of the office, past the security guys lounging lazily by the first floor entrance. A walk to Uhuru Park would clear my head. Fresh air, if one could find some in this city, was what I needed.

It was mid-morning and already the hustle and bustle of the city had begun in earnest. I crisscrossed my way down the busy Kimathi Street, across Uhuru Highway and into the park. I stopped briefly to light a cigarette, puffed on it and inhaled the nicotine-laden smoke, noisily sucking some air through my teeth. I looked at the tip of my cigarette, watching the ember glow and crackle as I flicked the ashes off with my finger. I felt a little light-headed but it was better than the throbbing that was pounding my temples like tidal waves trying to breach the bow.

After aimlessly wandering around the park for a while, I finally sat on a park bench near Freedom Corner, watching a mother duck and her brood gliding playfully in the pond, unaffected by the cacophony and smells around us.

I pulled on the last bit of my cigarette. I threw the stub down and snuffed it out on the dirt beneath my feet, twisting the life out of it. I coughed up a little sooty phlegm that was caught in my throat and quickly spat it out in front of me. It hit the ground with a muffed sound and instantaneously curled into a dusty ball, instantly concealing its identity. I needed to seriously think about quitting this habit, I told myself. These things will kill me.

Then I turned my attention to a group of teenage boys who were talking excitedly about the upcoming European Football League finals. One lanky youth cast a quick glance my way, sizing me up and then perhaps thinking better of it, letting out a long spit of saliva before resuming his part in the animated discussion. I watched them closely but without alarm, knowing that come what may I had to hold my ground. The city demanded this of you or some punk would try to jump you if you showed any weakness.

I pulled out the paper and laid it on my lap, opening out the sports section. Black and white portraits of members of the national soccer team stared back at me vacantly. They had taken another loss to Cameroon, a trend that was becoming quite embarrassing to the team and especially to the national coach, imported from Brazil. And then I turned over the pages back to King'ori's article.

What sort of man was he and how did he die? Why did Bulldog want this story investigated anyway? How well did he know King'ori, socially? What was King'ori like in private? As I juggled these and other questions in my head, it hit me! I could easily angle the story away from King'ori's death and look at other aspects of his life for something of interest. Or better yet, ferret out a secret or two. That was it! Bulldog would be a good starting point - he knew people. He must have even known King'ori. With that thought in mind, I got up and left for the office with forced alacrity but found Bulldog had already left for some meeting elsewhere.

All day I mulled over King'ori, trying this new angle. There were scanty details online about Takana Electronics but nothing really stood out. Most of the content with his mention was at fundraisers and around an annual golf tournament that his company sponsored. He did not have a Facebook account - well, neither did I! But I was slowly coming around to the idea. Social media was fast becoming a necessity.

Evening could not have come sooner. I had to re-examine my weekday beer binges, I told myself, as I went home and straight to bed. But the possibility of a political assassination kept on nagging me. Tomorrow I would be fresh and ready to work on King'ori's story.

Chapter Two

● ● ● ∙ ● ● ●

The next day King'ori's story was off the front page and it was no longer the lead on television and radio broadcasts. The obituary page carried a more somber picture of King'ori followed by a paragraph announcing the *untimely death of Mr. Isaac King'ori, son of the late Lucia and Jacaranda King'ori; loving husband to Jemima Waceke and Jennifer Murimi; father to Peter, Jane, Raymond, Absalom and Mary-Jane. Service and funeral arrangements to be announced soon.*

I looked at the notes I had so far gleaned from archives and online. King'ori had twice run for public office and twice had come up short. He then did the next best thing - put his vast wealth behind a surrogate who later returned the favour with handsome government contracts. Not much to go by but the outline of an ambitiously ruthless man who knew how to get things done his way was emerging. Even the way he came to own Takana Electronics, the giant appliance store on Kimathi Street, told of a single-minded and insidious approach to life. To begin with, his father, a potato farmer from Njoro, had loaned him all his life-savings to buy shares when Takana Electronics, where King'ori worked, went public.

According to the structure of its initial public offering, individual buyers were allowed no more than a thousand shares each. King'ori gave money to as many relatives and friends as he could gather, literally bringing them in busloads to Nairobi where they camped outside the banks which were selling Takana shares. They bought the maximum allowed under their own names but with the understanding that they would later transfer the shares to King'ori. One of his buyers had misunderstood the contract and later refused to convert the shares to him. Threats of bodily harm and much worse eventually made him give in but he had warned King'ori that every dog has its day.

It was rumoured that King'ori continued buying out shareholders, forcefully, and at less-than-market price. Lawsuits ensued. An internal audit and an investigation by the Revenue Office found no misgivings and the lawsuits were dismissed but not before, so rumour had it, many palms at the Revenue Office had been greased. Before his fortieth birthday, King'ori was named Managing Director and shortly after that, he bought out the Japanese interest in the company, which handed him majority ownership of the company.

King'ori acclaimed his success as a reward for his Christian devotion. He was a life-long member of the Lutheran Church to which he gave generously, especially to programs that helped women. "To whom much is given much is expected" he was fond of saying. His death must have been a shock to those who knew him as a devoted follower of Christ, who never missed a service or any opportunity to add to the church's coffers.

But to those who knew that he had stepped on many toes and necks on his way to the top, his death, I thought, could not have come as a surprise. It happened all the time - revenge is always a good motivator. One does not rise to such heights of wealth and power without making some serious enemies. But who of the offended would want him dead?

The night shift manager of the Days Inn, where King'ori was found dead, a round man with a bulging midsection, told the police that he had personally checked him in that evening. King'ori had asked not to be disturbed. There was nothing unusual about this request, he added. Most of their male patrons usually came with the expectation of privacy, especially when accompanied by or expecting female company. They called these arranged escapades *mpango wa kando*.

According to a police statement leaked to the media, it was the same manager who, shortly after midnight, found the door to King'ori's rented room on the second floor ajar. Poking his head in after knocking, he found the half-naked man on the bed. On realising that he was dead, he ran downstairs and called the police. King'ori seemed to have died from natural causes, perhaps a heart attack - a rich man's disease as the manager called it in his statement.

The first officers to arrive did not know what to make of the crime scene: no forcible entrance, no overturned furniture, no strewn papers or any other manifestations of foul play. They dusted for prints on the doors, windows, cabinets and headboard, toilet seat and anything else they came across. They carefully lifted the many prints and sent them off to the crime lab.

It was conceivable, I thought, that King'ori was caught up in this *mpango wa kando* lifestyle and that an irate husband or boyfriend had perhaps followed him or his partner there. But no one had been seen accompanying King'ori to his room and no one reported hearing or seeing anything suspicious. Besides, such crimes of passion were almost always extremely violent and messy. It could also have been a random robbery gone badly - but robbers are not meticulous. This one seemed cerebral, organised and carefully executed, leaving no trace of incriminating evidence. So whoever did this would have to be someone who knew what they were doing right from the start - a professional hit man. Too many episodes of Colombo, I smiled.

It was, of course, also conceivable that King'ori had taken his own life but that did not add up either. Why here? Why not at his home, in his car or in a parking lot? Something was amiss.

I walked over to the Days Inn, quite a distance from my office, hoping it would help me think. I was not sure what I was going to find but I needed to get a visual sense of the crime scene.

As expected, the street leading up to the Inn was sealed off by two police cars on each side and the sidewalk cordoned off with police tape. A uniformed officer stood guard in the middle of the street looking on with disinterested exertion - the late morning sun unforgivingly beaming down on him. The entrance to the Inn was a hive of activity with detectives from the CID headquarters going in and out. A swarm of reporters huddled together, listening to a police spokesperson, a small man with an equally thin head, who kept on reassuring them no stone would be left unturned in the investigation. But when asked by a reporter if he suspected foul play, he refused to confirm or deny - standard police protocol. Two women, who I quickly learned were King'ori's wives, stood behind the police officer, hands in front of them except when they brought them up to wipe a tear in the corner of the eye. I tried to read reality behind the show of sorrow. I had to dig into any crevice that I came across: such was the work of an Investigative Reporter.

King'ori had attended almost all public events with his two wives and their children, the picture of family harmony, but apparently the two were not such good friends in private. They argued often - each accusing the other of monopolising their husband's time or even alleging that one was plotting the downfall of the other so that she might finally inherit all the wealth. But why would any one of them want their husband dead? It did not add up but still, I could not discount anything or anyone, even the children. In my line of business, I had known people to do irrational things blinded by jealous rage or insatiable greed.

After the police spokesperson finished his briefing, King'ori's first wife, a stocky woman in her late fifties, spotting a black sweater and a matching skirt, spoke in hushed tones on behalf of the family. She asked that their wishes for privacy be respected during this their time of mourning. The second wife looked on, stoically, nodding her head occasionally as if it was choreographed.

I understood their dilemma: The fact that King'ori had been found nude in a motel room was not becoming for a family man and a Christian. But still, I was a little perturbed by the quiet manner in which they wanted the matter handled - much like the church had conveniently overlooked he was a polygamous man. There was an absence of rage that one would have expected to hear in their first public statement. I tried to have a word with each one separately, but they would have none of it. My visit to the Days Inn therefore did not yield much.

On my way back to the office, I finally decided to call Detective Ali. I had always counted on him whenever I needed help with some investigative pieces that involved police work. I informed him that I was working on King'ori's story and I needed some information. After a brief pause he asked me to meet him at his new house. He was about to have lunch with his wife but I was welcome to join them. I took the bus to Loresho and before long I was walking up his driveway.

Ali's house, an elegant brick bungalow, was tucked away in a quiet cul-de-sac off Lima Road. It was part of a new development complete with tree-lined sidewalks, trimmed bougainvillea hedges and flower gardens which added to the peacefulness of this glitzy Loresho neighbourhood. They had recently moved there from a nondescript three bedroom maisonette in Parklands. His wife, Fatima, a Real Estate agent, must have found this gem. What a lucky dog! I always felt a twinge of jealousy whenever I visited with them, even at their old house. They led a nice quiet life, not quite extravagant but very tasteful.

I rang the doorbell twice. The ding-dong was followed by footsteps and then the door opened. It was Ali. He leaned over and gave me a hug before ushering me in. He wore a white shirt, a red tie and tan khaki slacks. He was always smartly dressed, albeit conservatively, even when he was off duty. He was of medium build, five-eight but he appeared taller.

He and Fatima had been married for a while now and, two boys later, they still met for lunch at least once a week and went out on dates. They still giggled at each other and played little silly games, like footsies under the table, which Ali had told me was the secret to their happiness.

"Come in and make a plate, handsome," Fatima beamed from the dining table.

I went over to her and gave her a kiss on the cheek. I always wondered how she retained such youthful features.

"You must be working out," I said to her as I sat down.

"Twice a week," she said holding her hips and posing like a model.

She laughed softly and sat next to Ali who was now chowing down on some sautéed beef stew and rice.

"So, how are you - and please don't tell me you are still single?" Fatima started as soon as I had fixed a plate.

"There she goes again," Ali said with mock indignation.

"What? I keep telling him I will hook him up with some of my friends," she continued.

"Jack, trust me, I have met her friends; you don't want any one of them," Ali said with a mouthful. "Don't let her take you down that road. It's dark!"

"Oh, please, I will have you know that I have quite the skills to find him a match," she argued. "Just say when."

"Leave the man alone," Ali said, turning to me. "I'm sure he does not need your help."

He caught me looking at some automobile brochures on the floor and explained that he and Fatima were in the market for a new car. Thankfully, the discussion turned to automobiles. They had not yet settled on any make.

After lunch, Ali and I went outside for a smoke. We sat on some lounge chairs overlooking a beautifully tended yard, complete with a children's swing set.

"So how did it go last night?" I asked.

"What do you mean?"

"I'm talking about the other night - at Uthiru," I went on. I looked over at him and caught him staring at me.

"What?" I asked wondering if I had something on my face.

He smiled slyly, saying, "Is that where you guys went after Broadways? I left early, remember? You guys were having such a good time though. How did it end up?"

Oh yes. I slowly pieced together the events. We had met at Broadways Tavern, an interesting bar with a mixed clientele from the Estates, students from the Veterinary Laboratory, an affiliate of University of Nairobi and working class families along the Kangemi-Uthiru Road. Ali had asked us to find him at the Tavern because he was meeting there with someone from the Coroner's office and it would save him from having to drive all the way back into the city to meet us. When Otieno and I arrived, Ali was still in the meeting in a room reserved for private parties. So we sat at the counter and ordered some drinks. Shortly after we had downed two beers apiece, Mburu had joined us.

And then the manager of Broadways, a skinny man with an unheralded affinity for Shakespeare, walked over to us, and after warm handshakes proceeded to order a free round for the three of us before quoting some suspect Shakespearean verses.

It was only after he had finished with his guest that Ali joined us. After a few drinks and some roast goat, he left.

I pulled on my cigarette and decided against filling Ali in on the details: I wanted to talk about King'ori and not about our escapades in Uthiru.

"You know how Otieno is!" I said, vaguely.

"Yes, that Otieno is something else, man."

We finished smoking just as Fatima joined us briefly to admonish us for our bad habits. Ali looked at his watch and announced that it was time to head out.

We bade Fatima farewell. She gave me a playful lookover as she walked to give me a hug.

"We need to get you a good woman," she said, squeezing me in her arms. It felt good - I had not hugged a woman in a while.

"Say hi to the kids for me," I said after she had released me. After she and Ali hugged and kissed, we headed back to the city in his unmarked police car.

I had met Ali through Otieno. But our young friendship became severely strained after I started dating Zuleika, his younger sister. He disowned me as his friend, banished me from his presence and refused to take my calls. He also refused to talk to his sister to accentuate his disapproval of our courtship. I guess he took it that I had broken some sort of code that forbade friends from dating their friends' sisters. My relationship with Zuleika ended quickly, perhaps hastened by her brother's prodding.

When Ali found out that we were no longer dating, his hostility and silent resentment ended and we resumed our friendship as if nothing had ever happened. Even when we talked about past relationships, Ali and I never brought up my dating Zuleika. But even in this denial, there remained a mild tension between us - Ali always claiming that I was selfish and stubborn and I maintaining that he was one-track-minded and foolhardy. Quite often, Otieno was forced to mediate.

Ali had one endearing quality about him that, Otieno and I agreed, overrode his other shortcomings: he loved his family. If you got him started, he would talk endlessly and animatedly about his wife and their two sons, Abdi, 5, and Awale, 4. He enjoyed taking them on long rides to the country and for outdoor adventures or camping out in the National parks.

He and his wife, Fatima Zawadi, had met shortly after Ali graduated from the police academy in Kiganjo and after a brief courtship, they were wedded. Their children followed quickly even as Ali worked his way up the ranks: an intensely focused individual who went for something with single-minded purpose.

Fatima on the other hand was quite relaxed and displayed a free-spirited nature. But she doted on her husband and her children and although she worked part-time in Real Estate, she made it home before anyone else to make dinner and get the house in order. Watching them together, I often wondered what family life might have been for me if my father had stuck around. My mother and I had a very good relationship but that alone could not replace a sense of loss that came with not knowing my old man.

We drove a little way in silence and then Ali interrupted my thought flow.

"Say, what did you need help with, my friend?" he asked after we had joined traffic on Uhuru Highway.

I told him about my new assignment. He listened intently as I outlined what I already knew about King'ori, including the bit on polygamy.

"I'm not sure where or what I should be looking for but anything about King'ori; anything that the public is not privy to."

After a brief silence he asked, "How did you know that I have been assigned the case? Lead detective, as a matter of fact!" he added with a soft laugh.

I looked at him. His face was beaming with pride.

"Oh, man! I did not know. That's some good news. Congratulations might be in order, even in a murder case!" I said extending my hand.

I was really happy for him. This guy had everything going for him.

"Ah man! it's not a biggie," he said, smiling and then continued. "I should also congratulate you on being assigned a high profile case."

"I don't know whether that warrants any celebration - I hate murder cases."

"No one likes death but we both have a job to do; I investigate, you report."

"So, like I'm your sidekick - two amigos chasing the bad guys eh?"

"Not really but something like that." He smiled again. He was really enjoying his new position it seemed.

"Well, just give me the inside scoop, something I can sink my teeth into for a good read." I wanted to make sure that he understood I wanted this story. "I'll handle your leaks to the press and in turn you get me the exclusive on this one. And since you know more than what you brief us about officially, throw me a bone every now and then."

"I'll see what I can do for you," he conceded. "But we have to go unofficial: it's an on-going investigation."

I knew what he meant: if he gave me the scoop, I was not to quote him as the source.

As he dropped me off outside my office building, I asked him if he thought King'ori was murdered.

"You don't waste time, do you?" He laughed and shook his head.

I waited, thinking of a follow up question. He then cleared his throat and I turned to face him. His face was now somber.

"We are not ruling anything out this early," he said. "And you can quote me on that one."

CHAPTER THREE

● ● ● · ● ● ●

King'ori's funeral was not a small affair. President Joakim did not make it but he sent a personal emissary to deliver his message of condolences to the family. After the burial, I headed back to the office. I had not made any headway. The death was still a mystery and I began to wonder if he had not indeed died of natural causes.

In the early afternoon, I walked to Kenyatta Avenue for a quick lunch at Suku's Lounge, wondering if I could make a story from what Ali had told me the other day. But he had not told me anything new beyond what I had already got from the police briefings at the Inn. I suppose I could sensationalise the fact that Ali was the lead detective, but I was an investigative journalist, not a newshound.

I had joined *The Daily Grind* shortly after college. My journalism degree would finally pay off; I told my mother who had begged me to get an economics degree so I could land a well-paying job. In vain, I had tried to convince her that labouring day in and out at a job that one did not enjoy killed one's spirit.

"So we should just go through life without toil in order to keep the spirit alive?" she had asked with a resigned and disapproving look.

I knew where she was going with this. She had worked long and hard to give me a good living. My father, a drifter of sorts, had left us to find work in Mombasa soon after I turned five. He never came back. My mother told me that he had been bewitched by a veil-wearing temptress and that he had lost all his faculties. Stories of genies and mermaids luring many a man into the sweet nectars of this lazy Indian Ocean city abound. Being too young to understand any of it, I went about life hoping that the temptress would find occasion to let my father go, or better yet, that he would one day find the strength to escape and come back home.

So when news came to us, years later, that he had been found dead with stab wounds to his chest, I blamed it on the genies. At the funeral, I kept looking at all the women wearing veils, trying to find out which one was the genie that had killed my father. I was too scared to cry and, after the burial service at my grandmother's farm, I realised that I had no tears left for him. I did not really know him after all.

"Well, your father did what he loved, and look what it got him," my mother commented with finality.

I knew there was no way for me to counter that without seeing her face flood with sorrow, but I had to say something. It was not until I was much older that I learned the details of my father's demise.

In Mombasa, he had found work at a tourist resort as a gardener. It did not pay much and he worked long hours in the humid heat. The letters he wrote promised money in the weeks to come and after a while my mother just gave up and asked him to come home. Then the letters stopped coming altogether. He found a young Swahili woman to keep him company at night. He moved in with her and after a while she kicked him out after she found out that he was a married man and with very little to offer her despite his big talk of fame and fortune.

He lost his job at the tourist resort after quarreling with the landscaping supervisor over some missing petunias that were supposed to have greeted guests at the gate. He resorted to dumpster-diving for food and sleeping at friends' houses until they too got tired of him and kicked him out.

After years of humiliation and hard-luck, he had taken to petty theft and borrowing money he had no means or intention of paying back. It was one of his debtors who had stabbed him to death over a loan of a mere handful of Kenya shillings.

I do not think that my mother really understood my father's travails. There were times when I really wanted to let her know that he had not lived a glamorous life, that he had died a pauper. I never did. What good would that do? As far as she was concerned, he had abandoned his family and taken up with a temptress and that was all there was to it.

"Hey, what can I get you?" a voice asked me impatiently.

I looked up and saw a gangly waiter standing beside me, balancing a small round tray in his left arm while picking up bottles and plates from an adjacent table with the other. I was not sure he was addressing me but I ventured to order a chicken sandwich and a cup of tea. Without responding, he sauntered off towards the kitchen.

Suku's was not particularly my type of joint. Loud rap music imported from America boomed from wall-mounted speakers. Jay Z, the half-dollar rap-artist, Eminem, James Atwater, Eve and other American rappers raged about things I did not understand and some which I was not sure about or familiar with. The young clientele, adorning *"I Love New York"* jerseys, saggy bottom pants, Timberlands and Jordan sneakers, shook hands and threw signs with their fingers, mannerisms that were completely alien to me while scantily dressed young women flocked around them, laughing and giggling. Perhaps it was their casual and carefree manner that irked me but I had enough on my plate and my mind went back to King'ori's murder.

The waiter plopped my sandwich and tea on the table before me without saying a word. He then stood there waiting for me to pay up but I decided to pretend not to understand his body language. I meticulously rearranged the fixings on my sandwich, applied some ketchup and proceeded to eat with much pomp and ceremony. For a while the waiter stood his ground but gave up after I let out a nice loud belch. It was not the best chicken sandwich south of the equator but it would quieten the hunger pangs. I sipped on the tea. I could feel it wash down the chicken, nestling it down and warmly in my stomach.

Shortly thereafter, I paid up and took the short walk back to work. It was settling into another afternoon spent chasing leads that led me nowhere.

All seemed quiet again. But the evening news broke the calm. Dr. Juma Kizito had been found dead at Ndeiya Inn, Limuru. Another murder?

CHAPTER FOUR

The good doctor was a renowned medical researcher at the Kenya Medical Research Institute (KEMRI). He held patents for several HIV anti-retroviral drugs which many international drug companies had tried to persuade him to relinquish without success.

Dr. Kizito's numerous accomplishments in the medical field were well-documented. He was the first in his family to go to University where he graduated with a Bachelor's Degree in Biology. He was offered a teaching position at an international high school but he turned it down, opting to attend Yale Medical School in the United States.

He then completed residency training at Mt Sinai Hospital in New York City and at the behest of his mentor he pursued fellowship training in Infectious Diseases at Stony Brook University in Long Island, New York, where he stayed on for seven years and rose to the rank of Senior Researcher.

Dr. Kizito then made some major breakthroughs in the understanding of HIV and other viral infections which led the Mayor of New York to appoint him to chair a task force to combat HIV/AIDS in New York and the Tristate area. He was making quite a name for himself and his research institution which translated to more research dollars from endowments and other funding agencies. His appointment at KEMRI did not come as a surprise to many but it did cause serious trepidations at Stony Brook who understood well that they were losing a vital asset to their institution.

As the Director, Dr. Kizito had transformed KEMRI into the leading research center in East and Central Africa. His achievements and promise as a scientist notwithstanding, he was humble, benevolent, a great advocate for the delivery of preventive medical information using local clinics and free mobile units led by practitioners and other healthcare aides to rural Kenyan communities, arguing that it did not make sense for Kenya to produce research and knowledge that did not benefit her people.

Dr. Kizito heralded the first ever collaboration between KEMRI and local hospitals and dispensaries, a union that saw rapid improvement in medical services. More doctors and nurses could now easily access the latest technologies, medical practices and professional development training, all funded by KEMRI. On his death, Kenya had lost an intellectual giant, one often mentioned as a possible winner of the Nobel Prize in Medicine for his work on Immunology.

As the details of Dr. Kizito's death begun to trickle in the newsroom, there emerged a picture eerily reminiscent of King'ori's death. No bodily trauma, no forcible entry or puncture wounds - a carbon copy! Yet, I could not even begin to think of the slightest connection between the two men. It may well have been a coincidence, but my mind wrapped around the possibility of a copycat killer.

With that thought in mind, I grabbed my coat and ran to the door. Otieno came panting after me and we both boarded the first commuter bus to Limuru.

The bus was actually a diesel Nissan van converted into a minibus. It had more people than the legal limit of fourteen and I hoped that the ride would be without incident to add to our relative discomfort. It was not to be. As soon as we reached the Limuru road, the driver spotted two traffic cops signaling him to stop. He decided to make a run for it and came barreling through the road block. The police scrambled out of the way and into their vehicle to give chase. We did not get far. They pulled their car alongside the minibus and one of the policemen riding shotgun drew out his weapon and pointed it at the driver. He decided to stop. They pulled the driver out and dragged him towards the police vehicle, with him pleading his case. After some negotiations, the driver came back, smiling, jumped in and drove off, trying to make up for lost time, and money!

I was terrified, but with good reason. Once, as a boy visiting with my aunt in Kamirithu, I saw a *matatu* full of passengers and a Leyland truck ferrying corn to Uganda collide near Ngenia High School. We rushed to the scene. The mangled *matatu* was on its side with the surviving passengers crying and screaming for help. Some were pulled out of windows while others just lay there, dying or dead inside the van. A stream of blood formed quickly under it, meandering down the side of the road like a small river.

By the time the ambulance came, the river had all but dried up leaving a trail of coagulated blood that caked and cracked up under the sun. The dead were piled together like logs of firewood and covered with some old blankets and stained white sheets that soon blotted into a wet, crimson dye.

I shook my head trying to get these images from my mind just as Otieno turned and asked, "Say, what you think is going on?"

I felt little droplets of saliva land on my left cheek and I wiped them off quickly. With the music blasting from the speakers and Otieno showering me with spittle, I was not in the mood for loud conversation so I just looked at him, pointed to my ears and shrugged my shoulders.

He leaned over closer to me and repeated the question, even more loudly. I could feel him staring at me so I turned and yelled loudly into his ear that I could not understand a word he was saying. He jumped back, his ears obviously ringing, and that did the trick - he was quiet the rest of the way.

The Ndeiya Inn was surrounded by curious onlookers. Police had not cordoned off the entrance, but instead a burly policeman with a menacing scar on his face paced up and down the entryway which led to a flight of steps. We edged through the crowd, making our way to the front. Then we wiggled through to the door.

"Where do you think you are going?" asked the policeman.

I flashed my badge. It was really my work ID card that I had had laminated and it seemed to make an impression on the policeman. We stepped right in and walked upstairs.

At the bar area, located on the first floor, we ran into Ali. He acted all official as he walked us to a table by the bar and we all sat down. Plainclothes and uniformed officers darted in and out from the lodging area.

Everything looked in place. But for the fact that we were here because someone had died, it just seemed like an ordinary bar doing bad business. A pool table stood at the corner invitingly. I always associated pool tables with beer, but I thought better of it. 'Pool can wait,' I thought to myself, turning my attention to Ali who was talking:

"Dr. Kizito checked himself in unaccompanied, saying he needed the room for the rest of the evening. Not unusual - it happens all the time with business travelers, secret lovers and weary tourists looking for local excitement. The manager was operating with just a skeleton crew at the time, business being slow and all, so it would have been easy for someone to come in undetected. No one saw or heard anything untoward. When one of the workers found the door ajar, knocked at the door and got no response, he called the front desk with his cell phone. Dr. Kizito was found dead at 3 p.m."

Ali paused for a minute to pick something from the tip of his tongue. He looked a little flustered, as if the shine on the calm 'I-am-in-charge-demeanor' with which he had proudly told me of his having been appointed lead detective was wearing off. Two high profile murders with no murder weapon, no suspect, no witnesses or any kind of lead would unnerve the very best in the police business but it was shaping into a nice storyline for me.

"If this is a murder, whoever did this covered their trail very well," he continued, now looking around as if trying to find a clue on the walls that might open floodgates of evidence.

I listened carefully to what he was saying and not saying. I took note of his mannerism, choice of words and the gaps of silence between them. I found nothing in his summation of facts that cried foul play except that there was a dead scientist upstairs. I do not know what I was expecting from the briefing but it was a little disappointing that Ali had nothing to offer me.

Police work, it seemed, was always one step behind the crime and unless the criminal made some careless mistakes, the investigators had to rely on a guess and a prayer. They lifted finger-prints and small fibers from Dr. Kizito's clothing but no one expected that these items would yield any tangible results.

"Do you think this is related to King'ori's murder?" I ventured.

"It's too early to tell but we cannot rule anything out at this time," Ali replied after a brief pause that told me he had thought about it. He continued, "I personally don't see a connection but until we have tangibles, we cannot dismiss any possible angles. In cases such as these, we have to assume the worst. It eliminates any surprises later."

He was acting and answering me in his official capacity. Later, when I got a private moment with him, he would surely tell things that he could not say in an official briefing.

"Is suicide something you are also looking into?" Otieno asked.

"I said I am not ruling out anything. We work through a process of elimination."

"Is there any word from the Coroner's office regarding King'ori?" I asked quickly.

"No, they have not been able to ascertain the cause of death, but I will let you know as soon as I hear something," he said in a tone that seemed to assure me that I would be the first to know.

With that, he got up, smiled and left.

I looked at the pool table again and ordered two beers for Otieno and me. Something did not add up but I could not place my finger on it. I would have to talk to Ali tomorrow, and maybe he could fill me in, unofficially.

As we sat there drinking our beers in relative silence, a couple walked in, holding hands, followed by two young guys: one, tall, lanky and confident and the other one short and seemingly unsure. They looked like regulars and I was about to challenge Otieno to a pool game when I heard them mention Dr. Kizito.

"Yeah, they f-f-found him upstairs, man. It's cr-cr-creeping me out," the shorter of the two stuttered.

"Man, come on. How many people die in this town daily and I've never heard you say it's creepy?" his compatriot looked at him indignantly.

"I kno-kno-know but he d-d-died here last night!"

The bartender handed them their drinks, mechanically opened them and tossed the bottle tops in the trash bin directly behind him.

"Were you wo-wo-working here last n-n-night?" the shorter guy asked him.

"No," answered the bartender curtly, going to sit at the far end of the counter, away from the two. It was like he knew they were trouble.

"D-d-damn, what's with h-h-him?" the shorter guy asked, looking around to see if he recognised anybody.

Our eyes met briefly and I gave him a little nod. He turned away quickly without acknowledging me.

"Just leave the poor guy alone, man," the taller of the two said, took a swig of his beer, belched loudly and continued. "You know how the Doctor was with women. I would not be surprised if a husband offed him."

I knew that Dr. Kizito was quite the ladies' man. He was always photographed in Society pages with a different woman by his side. He had been voted most eligible bachelor by Pulse Magazine for two years running. I could not begrudge the guy, his good fortune, but married women were a whole other matter. I made a mental note to look at this possible liaison with some married woman as a motive for someone to kill him. On this, I agreed with Ali: I too could not rule anything or anyone out.

After a cold and crisp tusker beer, we decided to head back to the city.

The darkness outside, interspersed with dim lights from distant houses, reminded me we were driving through Red Hill, a community of rolling flower farms, polyurethane greenhouses and coffee plantations. We passed the neon billboards announcing Johnny's Flower Farm, Gordon Plantations, Ameri-house Holdings, Adam, Eve and Sons and others I could not pronounce. I always found these Euro-American inflexions quite disturbing since almost all of these farms were owned by Kenyans.

Otieno had barely spoken on our way back and even after we alighted from the *matatu* in Nairobi, we continued walking in silence. His demeanor had changed quite a bit ever since we got to Limuru. Perhaps all this was affecting him more profoundly than he let on. I turned to him.

"You ok, man?" I asked him as I lit a cigarette.

"Yeah, man. I'm just chilling."

We took a few more steps. It was most unlike Otieno to remain silent for such a long time. So I prodded him.

"What's on your mind, man?"

"I think the government must be involved in these killings," Otieno postulated.

"I highly doubt that," I said unconvincingly.

I could not get it out of my mind that King'ori had died the day after he had accompanied the President to an event.

"You don't think the government is capable of…." Otieno was persistent.

"That's not what I mean. I just think you are jumping way ahead of yourself."

"But it is a possibility. Any rising star, popular figure if you will, poses a threat to the current political bigwigs, especially when one is being recognised internationally as well."

Otieno liked to engage in philosophical arguments. He was also prone to conspiracy theories. As far as I was concerned, King'ori and Kizito posed no threat to the present government.

"That might have been true under dictatorial rule, but…"

"Are you suggesting that we now have a full-fledged democracy?"

"No, but we are making positive strides."

Otieno was a great guy. He could be playful, obnoxious even, but always personable. He was also very serious, especially when it came to work. He did a weekly column on social issues, touching on anything from health to poverty and even popular music. He would inject humour, satire and his own brand of wisdom. He had built quite a following.

"How's your wife?" I asked him as we crossed Muindi Mbingu Street, just to change the subject.

"She's ok, just trying to keep up with the kids …"

He and Akinyi had been married for over seven years and they had three children. Two were from Akinyi's previous marriage and the last born was theirs together. But to see them all together, you would not have noticed any difference. Otieno was a happy-go-lucky fella who did whatever he could for his family. She, on the other hand, was serious and soft-spoken. But she ran a tight ship at home. Otieno learned this the hard way.

One night he had walked to his home stark naked after being stripped off his clothing by thugs. His wife, on seeing her husband, let out a scream that pierced the night.

"Hey, what is this now? You go drinking and come home in your birthday suit? What example are you setting for your kids?" she yelled.

He tried to explain but she was not having it. She carried on until she had worked herself into a frenzy and then began to rain blows on him for all past, present and future misgivings. Defenseless, naked and drunk, Otieno ran out before his kids awoke. It was quite a spectacle, a naked drunk man being chased with a broom by his wife, who with amazing dexterity was able to land several loud thwacks on his buttocks as he staggered across the lawn. By now, most of the neighbours were witnesses to the spectacle.

Otieno hid out in a ditch until his wife had gone to work early in the morning. Covering his dick and his sore buttocks with some wet cardboard that he had found in the culvert, he sprinted back to his apartment. He later explained his plight to an apologetic wife and order was restored in his household. But it became a running joke amongst his friends who teased him for the manner in which his wife had dispensed swift justice to his naked behind - he had received what we now called an 'Otieno' in his honour.

They had come to a sort of understanding: he could have his drinks but must make sure his after-work activities did not ever disgrace her or their household.

"Let's stop for a drink," I suggested.

From here it was easier to get home than from the Limuru. Going the final distance did not require too much planning. One of the vagaries of public transportation was that you had to plan drinking around the bus schedule and the time it took to walk home from the bus station. You did not want to be out late at night without risking being 'Otieno-ed' by thugs. Danger lurked all around Nairobi and the surrounding metropolis, waiting for you to drop your guard for just an instance. But it always felt good to be in Nairobi.

"Where?" Otieno asked, meaning he did not object.

"The New London Grill."

"Now you are talking!" he said, immediately picking up the pace.

CHAPTER FIVE

The New London Bar and Grill was an elegantly somber joint, with dimly lit candescent lights hanging from the high ceilings. The walls wore muted and sanguine beige colours where large paintings of European men on horseback were displayed in all their majestic grandeur. On the far right, towards the main dining area, was the picture of the queen, shaking the hands of what appeared to be an African child.

The Grill, despite its strong affinity to things British, served up mostly local fare, from *nyama choma*, to *githeri*, a mixture of kidney beans and corn, sautéed with shallots, garlic and served over rice *pilaf*. But they also had their international menu that catered for western palates that were not yet ready for African cuisine.

Truth be told, it was not really the food or the proximity to the bus stop that made me suggest this place. I also wanted to see Meredith, a waitress who worked the evening shift. She had a pretty face on her, the kind of girl that grows on you over time. I was quite taken by her but I did not have the courage to make a move, so I would always say a polite hello and nothing more whenever we came in for drinks.

That, until one day when I was shooting pool with Otieno, some tourist motherfucker challenged us to a game. He was a white man, an American, judging by his accent, and there was something about him I did not like.

"I'll play anyone up in here for twenty dollars a game," he sang, shaking his shoulders up and down for no reason at all.

He pulled out a wad of notes and slapped a cool twenty dollar bill on the table. He was smiling, his eyes dancing in the light with self-importance.

"Take him out, Jack," Otieno said.

He knew I had a good stick on me. I racked the balls on the table and I let him have three games before I raised the stakes to fifty dollars a game and then I laid it on him. Four hundred dollars later, he smiled and acknowledged that he had been hustled. I did not argue with him as I pocketed my earnings.

Otieno walked over to the shamefaced tourist and patronisingly placed his arm on his shoulders.

"How would you say that lesson went?"

The tourist, his eyes narrowing in anger, was about to say something but on looking around decided that numbers were clearly against him. After we sat down for drinks, Otieno was laughing so hard that he fell off the chair. Meredith came over to bring our drinks.

"You really play well," she said.

I smiled at her, trying to keep my eyes on her face. Otieno straightened up, wiping tears from his eyes.

"You should have seen him back in the day."

"You hustle pool all the time?"

"I'm a journalist who just happens to have good eyes and good hands," I answered. "Do you play?"

She faked annoyance and said, "Oh, now you want to hustle me?"

"We can make it a friendly."

"I'm not going to play against you, not after that display!" she said playfully. "I'm glad you took him out though. You made him pay for his arrogance."

And thus we began to get to know each other.

From the little tidbits I gathered every now and then, I learnt that she had moved here from Nyeri to stay with a boyfriend who promised to help her enroll at the Kenya Polytechnic University College to study Catering Management. He kept his word and for a year he provided for her while she attended school. Then one day he declared that he no longer wanted her in his life. Just like that, no reason given - it had to be something to do with another woman.

Luckily, one of the instructors at the Poly arranged for a place for her to stay in. Every now and then, he would check on her to make sure that she was doing okay. But one night, the 'Good Samaritan' came in drunk and demanded to be 'paid.' She refused and threatened to tell his wife. He stopped paying the rent. In this city, there was nothing for free, she realised, but she was determined to continue with her classes. Then she found work at the New London Grill as a dishwasher and then waitress.

Making ends meet became a struggle but working for tips at the New London enabled her to pay rent and also pay her school fees. The manager, a guy called Ben, had shown her the ropes, patiently and without the unsavoury demands she had come to expect of anyone being nice to her. I liked her tenacity and upbeat nature despite the hardships she had encountered in the city.

That's why, after the events in Limuru, the New London Grill was a welcome sight. We walked in like men on a mission. Our usual booth was taken but Otieno looked around and found an empty table. I turned my gaze to the counter, looking for Meredith, who waved. I waved back before joining Otieno, who by now had rolled up his shirt sleeves like one getting ready for manual labour. He had that grin on his face now and I knew he was alright.

"You guys might want to get something to eat," Meredith said. "Beer alone cannot be good for you."

I looked up at her. She smiled - her eyes lighting up.

"Sure. After the first round, I will get something," I replied. "What do you recommend?"

"I know you are getting the usual, so don't even try!"

Irio, a mixture of corn, peas and potatoes mashed together and served with slow-cooked beef stew with a side of steamed carrots deglazed with sherry and vinegar, was my favourite.

Otieno was ogling at her.

"And you, my good sir, what will you have?" she asked him after he had finally come up to breathe.

"What I want I can't have so I'll have a cold one," he said, his grin now breaking into laughter as she playfully hit him with a dish rag.

"I'll make sure you eat before you go home," she said, looking at me.

"You sound like my mother," I teased her.

She laughed and walked away saying that she would bring my order as soon as it was up. I watched as she tended to some other customers and I realised that I was still smiling.

I had had no luck with women ever since Linda, my girlfriend of six years, broke up with me. It had shocked me. I was in love with her and I had not seen it coming. 'We needed be alone for a while,' she had said. I wallowed in pain, anger and acrimony but to my friends, I maintained a level-headedness that belied what I was really going through. I do not know if she was already seeing him at the time of our breakup, but she married a lawyer not long after. It hurt. I decided to stay celibate for at least six months to heal. Six months had turned into a year and then another even after I recused my celibacy vows. Two years later, I was still single and celibate.

From time to time, I had dated, but never past a second meeting. Truth of the matter was that I was scared of abandonment. I knew, deep down, I did not want to be alone. I knew that I would sooner or later have to face up to my fears, but I was just not in a hurry. All I needed was time, opportunity and the right woman. My eyes were now on Meredith: and I felt good about her.

I do not know at what point Otieno brought back our experience of the day. He was relentless in his belief that Dr. Kizito's death was somehow connected to his rising popularity, a political assassination.

"Who gets to gain from his death? That is the question that will lead us to the motive," I insisted.

"You, my friend, are truly naïve," Otieno said as if he knew a thing or two but did not elaborate.

Well-fed and several beers later, we bade Meredith farewell with a generous tip, and boarded our bus to Dagoretti Corner. The neighbourhood where we lived comprised of all manner of buildings in various stages of construction - with materials ranging from brick and mortar to timber and cardboard, scrap metal and dilapidated tin. Men and women entrepreneurs in this locality bought and sold all kinds of cheap toys, scarves, hairbrushes and condoms from China. Dotting the shopping center and roadsides were makeshift butcheries, bars, eateries, and fruit-stands that boasted edibles from the hinterland.

It was not a bad place to live but the huge corrugated-metal gates and high stone fences lined with sharp shards of glass were a constant reminder that security was an issue. The houses looked like prisons, with windows spotting metal grid lattices and grates while the doors were reinforced with metal grills.

On arrival at our stop, Otieno dashed to a café to buy some chewing gum while I waited for him by the roadside. He always chewed on some gum before going home. There were still people hanging out at the bus stop, some hurriedly trying to get home while others were trying to get some food from the café.

"Alright man, I'll see you tomorrow," I said to Otieno when he got back.

"I think Meredith likes you," he said.

"What do you mean?" I asked, just to make him say it again.

"Don't pretend, man, you know she likes you," Otieno said as he walked away.

Before I could respond, a *matatu*, with loud music playing pulled up at the stop. Quickly, the passengers alighted and the *matatu* took off. I saw two of the passengers, one tall and one short, talking animatedly to the kiosk owner where Otieno had just bought his gum. Was it just a coincidence or were they the same ones from the Ndeiya Inn? Was I becoming paranoid? No, it could not be. People were always haggling over something, I thought, and left for home.

That night I was about to doze off when my phone rang. I answered. There was no response. The caller ID showed unavailable. I put the phone down and just as I pulled the covers to my head, it rang again - still no response. Hmm!

CHAPTER SIX

● ● ● · ● ● ●

The next morning, I headed for Dr. Kizito's home at Kikuyu. I was not sure what I would find but there was something; call it journalistic curiosity or a penchant for a story, pointing me to that direction. I was never one to sit idly around, waiting for a story to unfold. I was a go-getter.

Kikuyu, five miles from Nairobi, is home to the famed Sigona Golf and Country Club, KEMRI, and Alliance High School for Boys and another for Girls. In fact, Otieno Kibogoye and Ali Fana, both young boys from Buru Buru, had graduated from the boy's school with big dreams leading them into the world.

The bus driver seemed to be making his own rules, dashing in and out of traffic, and honking wildly as he zoomed past other cars. Oncoming motorists and pedestrians had to scamper out of his way. I was holding on to my seat for dear life, staring wide-eyed ahead.

I asked him to slow down. The other passengers seemed unconcerned and looked at me like I was crazy for asking. It was as if they had resigned their lives to fate.

They say that there are many ways to die but I did not want some lunatic driver to dictate my exit. I demanded he drop me off at the next stop where I took another bus.

Dr. Kizito's house was quite impressive. A nicely manicured lawn divided by a cobblestone driveway that meandered to the main house. I was surprised that he did not have a gate as is common amongst the very wealthy. The elegant landscape and the flower gardens pulled ones' eyes over to a picnic table that sat quietly under the canopy of a jacaranda tree. The main house was a two-storey bungalow with a huge patio overlooking a large pond complete with lilies and a water fountain.

I knocked on the front door and, when after a brief moment a woman opened the door, I introduced myself as a reporter and flashed my badge. There was really no need for me to flash it but I was getting used to flickering it open with one smooth move. I guess I had watched too many episodes of Law and Order.

"I thought you are with the police," she said as she ushered me in.

She was wearing a black dress with white stripes running down the length of it which made her appear taller than she really was. She had a pretty face - quiet but pretty. I extended my hand to greet her but I guess she did not see it for a while. So I awkwardly waved it in front of her to draw her attention. She apologised quickly after noticing her *faux pas*, taking my hand with both of hers. They were soft, obviously not used to hard labour.

"My name is Irene. I am Dr. Kizito's sister."

She let my hand go, slowly, drifting from her softness. Then she led me into the house.

"I don't live here," she said, turning around to face me. She then pointed to the chair in front of me and I sat down.

"I am home on vacation from Houston, Texas."

"Oh, I see. How are things in Houston?" I asked more out of decorum than curiosity.

She did not respond immediately and I thought that perhaps she had missed my question. I let it slide, knowing that she was under much sorrow and not in the mood for chit-chat.

"What can I do for you, Mr Chidi?"

Her pretty face, now burdened by grief, made me feel stupid for coming to bother her but I was here now and despite the unpleasantness, I had a job to do.

"I am so sorry for your loss," I said, with a sincerity that surprised me.

"Thank you," she answered almost in a whisper.

I could see tears well up in her eyes but she fought back, holding her hands tightly across her chest. Her cheeks quivered with sadness and all I could do was sit there, wondering what would be the prudent thing to say or do under the circumstances.

I looked around, thinking of something to say, and how to weigh the words so that I would not upset her. Thankfully, she came to my rescue with an offer.

"May I get you some water, or some tea?" she asked.

"Yes, please, some water would be just fine. When did you come in from Houston, Texas?"

"I have only been here for two weeks. My brother and I are going … were going to Mombasa for a week before I returned to my husband and children. Now, instead, I will be burying him."

She began to cry. I was still lost for words, not sure how to console her. I stood up and took the glass of water from her shaking hands. We sat down again and I waited for her to compose herself. I placed my hand on her shoulder gingerly. She was so soft and I found my mind wandering off to places it should not. I had not held a woman this close in years.

"I know it's hard, Irene," I said sincerely despite my brief moment of tenderness.

I pulled my hand from her shoulder hoping that I had not left it there too long.

"I'm sorry," she sobbed. "It's just so hard to believe that he is gone."

"I didn't mean to upset you," I said with trepidation, waiting for her to say something but when nothing was forthcoming, I continued. "I am here to ask you for a favour. I know you are hurting and I am so sorry to have to ask you to help me but I will understand if you are not so inclined."

With that, I paused and I looked at her but I did not sense disapproval, so I continued.

"Let me assure you first that nothing you tell me will go to print without your knowledge and permission. The reason I am here is because I think there is a link between your brother's death and that of Isaac King'ori a few days ago."

"Yeah, I read about that," she said softly, "but I don't see what that has to do with my brother."

"The police also don't seem to think so but there are glaring similarities that lead me to suspect that there is something going on here."

I was not sure that there was a connection but I had to give her something. If I needed to gain her confidence, I would have to tell her what I knew without reservation, so I laid it on her.

I told her all I knew about King'ori. She listened intently, watching my face as I spoke. There was something very sensual about her, I thought to myself. I tried to ignore these racing thoughts in my head with very little success.

She looked straight ahead in deep thought. I sipped on my water, waiting for her to process what I had just told her. Then she let out a huge sigh and said:

"I just don't understand why anyone would want to hurt my brother."

"Is there anything that you can tell me about your brother's demeanour these past few days? Was he seeing anyone? Any strange phone calls, things like that?"

I waited. She shook her head, then wiped her eyes with a Kleenex, sniffling.

"I have already told the police everything. There was nothing unusual about him. He seemed as happy as a lark when he left in the morning. In fact, I thought he was at work all day. He never mentioned that he was going to Limuru and I'm sure he would have called me since we grew up there."

"Perhaps something came up," I said sheepishly.

I wondered about his peers at KEMRI. Could anyone of them have wanted to have him removed? How about his patents? Who would benefit from his demise? The beneficiaries would have a motive. Perhaps this is where I needed to look. Who else stood to gain from this? I pried. I knew I was deep-sea fishing without gear but a drowning man will clutch at straws, I consoled myself.

"What about his colleagues? Did he ever say anything to you about his workplace? Anyone he did not get along with or someone who was jealous, anything you can think of, no matter how small?"

She was quiet for a second, thinking. Then she looked at me and averted her eyes.

"Not really …" she said haltingly.

I noticed a hesitation but did not know what it meant.

"Please, anything at all," I begged.

She was searching or perhaps wondering whether she should tell me whatever it was she had in mind. I was not sure if I should prod on or just wait. In this business, you had to know when to be pushy, hard-headed, nosy or just plain quiet. There was no formula but you could lose the confidence of your source by being impatient.

"I'm not sure this means anything but there was a company in Laredo, Texas, that had hounded him for a while."

"In the States?" I asked quickly.

Somehow, I had wanted this to stay local.

"Yes, Laredo, Texas in the USA," she repeated for emphasis. "Abscor Pharmaceuticals is the name," she almost exclaimed, as if she had suddenly recalled it.

"What did they want?"

"They were trying to buy his patents for anti-retroviral drugs. He had asked me to check them out for him because he did not want to do business with some start-up company with questionable credentials."

I had heard scary stories about the lengths pharmaceutical companies would go to in order to keep their monopolies of life-saving drugs from competitors. It was big business and if one drug cornered the market, the patents could allow them anything up to fifteen years of unfettered profits.

"What did you find?"

"This company did not have the best reputation as far as pharmaceuticals go. I told my brother about a case I saw online about Abscor and some clinical trials they had done on human subjects in the Honduras."

I was horrified at what she told me. Apparently Abscor scientists, with funding from the United States National Institute of Health, (NIH) collaborated with Honduran researchers to conduct gene-therapy trials on patients suffering from the genetic disorder, muscular dystrophy. To convince the Honduran government that their product was ready for human subjects, they cited several successful experiments they had conducted using mice. Twenty deaths occurred before the Honduran government banned the trials pending further investigations into adverse effects of the treatment.

Subsequently, it was discovered that Abscor had not obtained informed consent from the patients in the study. They had also deliberately failed to disclose pre-trial evidence that had shown poor efficacy of the treatment on baboons and Rhesus monkeys. That was why their protocols were on hold in the United States pending review by the NIH.

In a push to avoid long delays in getting their gene-therapy drugs to market, they had simply shipped their trials to Tegucigalpa, the capital of Honduras. Corporate interest in gene-therapy technologies and promises of massive profits had outweighed medical ethics and overshadowed public safety.

When the scandal broke out, Abscor stepped in unrepentantly and proclaimed that they owned the discoveries made on the clinical trials in Honduras without as much as acknowledging that they had violated medical ethics or even taking responsibility for the deaths. They sold all future discoveries to another private company pursuing gene-therapy technology for hundreds of millions of dollars. They also never compensated the victims.

"So my brother refused to work with Abscor but they did not stop there. He told me that they sent representatives to come and talk him into working with them."

She sat back, her face somber as if reflecting on what she had just told me. The room was quiet. In the distance, I heard a donkey bray, followed by a barking dog and then the sounds faded into the morning.

I did not want to interrupt her train of thought but this was taking a turn I had not expected. This was a good story in and of itself! I felt a little guilty at my rising excitement.

"They offered him all kinds of incentives, including money and Abscor shares but he would not hear of it," she went on unprompted.

"These people, did they talk on the phone or they actually sent representatives here?" I asked, unable to contain myself anymore.

"They came here," she said, paused and then, "Oh my god!" she began to cry. "You don't think…?"

"Now, now," I consoled her, "Let's not jump to conclusions but we can start looking at that angle."

My mind was racing ahead. Maybe they paid him and he reneged on their deal. There was only one way to find out how deep he was in Abscor: follow the money trail.

"Can you find out if any money ever exchanged hands?" I asked.

"What do you mean?"

"We need to see if they ever paid him any money in order to corner him into some bad deal."

Such dealings coupled with bribery or blackmail usually ended up in murder.

She wiped her face with a Kleenex and blew her nose loudly. I waited for her to compose herself. Eventually, she agreed to check her brother's accounts and business papers to see if there was anything for us to follow up on. In return, I promised to dig up more on Abscor and their Kenyan connections. Detective Ali, I assured her, would be very interested in this and he had the resources to investigate it fully.

I was strangely ecstatic. I was not sure how his death connected to King'ori's though it occurred to me that it might have been a copycat killer - possibly one hired by Abscor to throw off any investigation from pointing in their direction. That made a perfect cover.

She saw me to the door. I handed her my business card before I left, in case she remembered anything else. I would have wanted to stay with her longer but I had things to do. She had a gentleness that rose above her sorrow. I thought about Meredith. She had the same effect on me.

When I got back to the office, I poked my head into Otieno's cubicle. He was on the phone, and from his muted pleas, I knew it was Akinyi on the other end. He never seemed to learn and I never seemed to help his cause since we were always drinking together. I was about to walk back to my desk when he said, "Hold on, Jack." And to Akinyi, "Honey, I have to go. But I'll make it up to you, I promise."

"Still in the dog house eh?" I laughed heartily.

He looked at me and resolutely assured me that he wore the pants in his household. Then he flashed his usual grin but it did not carry its usual confident look.

"Yes, you are, Sir Otieno, yes you are!"

"Let's go for a smoke," he said and we walked out.

We ended up at a corner café not too far from the office. I toyed with the idea of an iced coffee but I asked for hot tea instead. Otieno ordered a cup of black coffee and buttered toast.

"So," I started after the waiter brought our beverages, "I met up with Irene, Dr. Kizito's sister."

"What is she like?"

"Jesus, man, the woman is mourning," I protested.

"I don't mean anything by it. I just want to know what she looks like, that's all."

"Ok, she's alright, man. But listen. She has an interesting theory about her brother's death. She thinks it has something to do with intellectual property rights. Dr. Kizito held quite an array of patents, you know."

I saw Otieno's eyes brighten but I was not sure if it was from the news or the huge sip of his coffee.

"Does she have any one in mind?"

"She told me about a company called Abscor."

"Why, did her brother work for them?"

"No, on the contrary, this company had quite an interest in Dr. Kizito's work."

I paused to have a sip. I told Otieno how they had pursued him and even offered him a huge buyout for his patents. When he turned that down, they sent a team of doctors and researchers to convince him to work for them but he was not interested.

"What do you mean he turned down a patent buyout? What was the figure?"

"I am not making this up. Abscor really wanted to get a hold of his patents but I guess Dr. Kizito knew they were worth much more than what they were offering. Do you know how much money these pharmaceutical companies make off drugs?"

"So what you are saying is that he was offered like a million dollars and he turned it down?" Otieno said, still musing over the huge offer.

"Yes. Perhaps he was asking for more. Who knows? But the larger point is that he refused to sell and these companies are known to do some really shady things to get their hands on what they want."

I reminded Otieno of that infamous case in India where a pharmaceutical company had tried to persuade two Indian doctors to sell patents for an anti-malarial drug that had shown promise during trial phase. The doctors refused. Six months in, they were both dead. An investigation later found out that a known mercenary had been hired by the pharmaceutical company to persuade them - well, so much for negotiations. Although no one was formally charged with the murders, the company settled out of court with the government, while denying any responsibility, and they got the patents.

"It can get very dangerous out there when it comes to drug money," I said wittily, "and these companies are very competitive. Whoever owns the product basically owns the market and whoever …"

Otieno interrupted my whimsical flow of thought.

"I was reading about bio-piracy the other day," Otieno offered. "It seems to me that very soon our very own plants and trees will belong to some foreign company. But do you think that it's possible to patent life?"

"If someone did, you would have to pay to procreate," I answered, trying to avert another prolonged debate with Otieno.

"That would make the life-patent holder the pimp-daddy of the world!" Otieno laughed loudly at his own joke.

"You are a fool, man. Let's get back to work, you pimp-daddy you."

We finished our drinks and headed back to the office. Irene had opened another dimension to the investigation. It was time to talk to Ali about what I had found out with the hopes that he too had more information for me.

CHAPTER SEVEN

Instead of calling Ali, I decided to go straight to his office at CID Headquarters located on Kiambu Road. I walked right through the gate, past a distracted or unconcerned security guard. In the building, I called the elevator but it delayed so I decided to walk up the stairs. Halfway through, my lungs reminded me why I should always take the elevator. I was thirty-three and already feeling like an old man from two bad habits - drinking and smoking. Sooner or later, I would have to give up one or both.

I panted up the remaining steps. Outside Ali's door, I took a few minutes to regain my composure. It is moments like this that reminded me that I needed to reactivate my gym membership.

I had boxed quite a bit in college and had done well in my weight class, out-boxing almost everyone who went up against me. My dream of vying for the Nairobi Regional Boxing Championship belt was cut short by Omondi, a young man from Kisumu, who took me to school with his hand speed and superior boxing skills. My friends, who had come to see me enter greatness, left even before the fight was over. Humiliated and hurting in places that I did not know existed, I quit boxing the next day.

Perhaps with a few rounds and hard work, I could reclaim my lost healthy body. Or better yet, I could take up swimming, or tennis, anything that did not require physical contact with any able-bodied human.

The secretary smiled automatically and I extended my hand in greeting. She had slender forearms that looked like candlesticks, but she had a firm grip. I liked that.

"I'm here to see Detective Ali Fana, he is my friend," I added the caveat lest she went back to check with him and then tell me he was gone for the day.

She stood up from behind her desk methodically, pulled at her skirt to straighten it as she walked past me and into the adjacent office. She was pretty but her makeup, which she applied liberally, made her look more like a porcelain doll than a budding beauty queen. I heard whispered instructions and she quickly came back to where I was standing. She stopped in front of me, smiling but not saying a word, with her hands held in front of her.

"Come in, my friend," Ali called from the door. "I see you have already met Joyce, my secretary."

"Yes, I have," I said. "Thank you," I added, nodding to her.

It was the first time I had set foot inside this building since their small unit of Homicide detectives were moved from Ufundi House after the 1998 US Embassy bombing. I was a little surprised at how bare his office was. I had expected photos, diplomas, a detailed map of the city with red pins marking areas of crime, you know, your standard sleuth's office. But the only photo hanging on the brown back wall directly behind his chair was that of President Joakim with eyes that followed your gaze no matter where you were seated or standing.

On his desk was a behemoth of a computer, hardly state of the art. Beside it was an equally huge and ancient printer that hummed incessantly for no apparent reason. A picture of Ali's wife, Fatima, and their two kids was neatly angled for the visual benefit of both himself and his visitors. That and the name on the door were the only identifiers of the occupant.

"How is it going, brother-man?" I asked after I sank into a chair facing him.

He smiled and leaned back, twirling a Biro ballpen in his right hand.

"Nothing, really, just trying to catch up with some paper work," he answered nonchalantly.

I deliberately pulled out my pen and note book.

"You and your note book! I thought this was a private visit, my friend!"

"Just a few questions, if I may. You know how it is," I mumbled as I opened my note book.

Then I looked up at him. He was still smiling, which signaled to me that it was ok to proceed.

"Have you received any new information? Any lucky breaks in either case?"

"No, no new developments," he smirked. "It takes time to get all the right dots to connect but we are working hard on it."

"What about the medical office's reports?" I asked, jotting down quickly on my pad.

"We have nothing official so far," Ali answered. "I was with the Coroners just the other day and they are still processing. We need them to move a little faster."

I waited for him to continue but he did not. I had no follow up question and so I flipped through my notes, trying to come up with one.

"Do you think that the deaths of King'ori and Dr. Kizito are related?" I asked.

"I have not seen the official toxicology report yet," he replied. "We should have that any time now. We are still investigating these two cases as unrelated since we do not have reason to believe that they are connected."

He was evidently giving me that official humdrum.

"Can I quote you on that?" I asked.

"Sure. We really have no basis to tie the two." He was still twirling his pen in between his fingers.

"But they both died the same way. I mean the *MO* is the same. Surely, you must think there is a connection despite the lack of evidence," I retorted.

"I cannot speculate. I have to go with facts. We have no motive, no killer, no weapons and no prints…nothing!"

He paused for a minute, looked outside his window and then continued.

"It's frustrating but without facts, concrete proof or tangible evidence, we have no case….just another dead bugger, a grieving family, a worried public and an agency badly in need of a break."

"I spoke with Irene, Dr. Kizito's sister earlier today…"

"Oh yeah, the Doctor's sister from Oregon!" he said raising his eyebrows.

"Actually from Houston, Texas," I corrected him.

"She is quite something, isn't she?" he smiled as if to divert my attention to the fact that he had the State wrong. "Man, I felt so bad for her. Here on vacation and it turns out to be a funeral. So what did you talk about?"

"She had a very interesting theory about her brother's death."

That caught his attention and he sat up. So I told him about Abscor. I could not discern the look on his face. It was as if he was ticked off that Irene had not mentioned this to him but at the same time relieved that this might be the break he had been looking for. I felt a little satisfaction for having brought such a pertinent piece of information to a detective.

"Well, what do you think?" I asked, trying hard not to rub it in.

He did not congratulate or openly acknowledge my good work, but he obviously took it seriously and, for a moment, was deep in thought, judging by the slight frown on his face. Then he stood up and paced back and forth. I could see the wheels turning.

"It is definitely an interesting angle," he said at last. "Abscor would have motive. Wow, this could be huge! This is good, my friend, this is good work. Did she say anything else?"

"That was pretty much it," I said, smiling.

He sat down.

"I think you might have something there," he consented. "We will need to talk to her some more. I can see how one can make that case. We will definitely look into it. Let's find out more about Abscor."

With that, he picked up his phone and dialed a number.

"Yeah, it's me. Can you meet me in fifteen minutes? We might have something worth looking into."

He then hung up and I was afraid he was about to dismiss me without indicating any further cooperation. I felt something inside me jump but I maintained my cool and when he stood up and grabbed his jacket, I thanked him for his time. Then he said we could all meet up for a drink later on. I was all for it and I was sure Otieno would too.

"I hope you and Otieno will keep it under control," he said with a smile. "And please, don't hesitate to call should you come across any other tidbits. I am not of course asking you to do my work, but anything helps."

I left, walking past the gate with the unconcerned guard still on duty. I realised that I had given more than I got from Ali, but that was to my credit. I smiled to myself, knowing that he now owed me. This was a crazy business and every favour owed was a good asset - it always paid dividends sooner or later.

* * *

Early the next day, my phone rang. I hoped it was not the same unavailable number from the night before. It was Otieno. The only time he had phoned me at this forbidden hour was when his wife had asked him to leave after a fight over some unpaid bills. It was an exile that usually lasted three days. What trouble was he in now?

"Man, what do you want this early?" I asked, reminding him about my rule of never receiving calls before 7 am or after 11 pm.

He cut me short:

"There's been another murder!" he thundered. "A professor was found dead at the Waldoria. I am headed there right now."

CHAPTER EIGHT

The Waldoria, located in the city center, was a plush hotel that was originally built in the 1930's but had since been renovated and updated several times into a world class outfit. I got there within the hour and found Otieno standing outside the cordoned off area talking with a uniformed officer. I shook their hands and pulled out my note book. Then I fumbled for my pen in my jacket but could not find it.

"Hey, man. What's going on? What happened?" I asked Otieno.

The uniformed officer looked me up and down and then giggled. I almost smacked that stupid smile off his face. Perhaps he needed to know who I was before he could divulge any information. So I pulled out my badge and flashed it. He ignored my badge.

"So you journalists do not zip up your pants?" he asked wryly and turned away.

I looked down and noticed that I was wide open. In my haste to join Otieno, I had forgotten to put on some underwear. I turned around quickly and zipped up. I tried to cover up my embarrassment by cracking a crude joke about going commando but he was no longer interested.

"From what I have gathered so far," Otieno briefed me, looking at his note pad, "they found him this morning, a Linguistics don, Professor Justin Obo ... "

My heart sank. I knew of Prof. Obo during my days at the university. I had not taken any classes with him but I had attended several of his lectures. He was quite an orator and everyone I knew liked him. He was married to a beautiful woman, Anna Obo, whom he always introduced as the "apple of his eye." Why would anyone want to kill him?

"Let's go in," I beckoned to Otieno.

The uniformed officer, still wearing that smirk on his face, let us through without any hassles.

The lobby was a lavish and immaculate display of French décor. But mounted on the wall behind the concierge's counter were two large African shields adorned with bows and arrows. A large banner welcomed the weary traveler with a bold exclamation: *The African jungle begins with a good night's sleep.* Underneath it was a picture of a white couple, dressed in wide brimmed hats, shorts and Nikon cameras hanging from their necks, pointing excitedly at some lions that were tearing up a gazelle. Behind them, a Masai warrior, bedecked in full battle regalia stood guard.

The lobby looked elegant, complete with soft leather couches and a coffee table laden with imported fruits, European niceties and a stack of International newspapers. At the far end of the counter stood a huge glass shelf with all sorts of brochures and travel guides but one in particular caught my eye. It announced a private tour of the city slums!

The Maître d'hôtel, a short stocky man wearing an over-starched tuxedo, was talking excitedly with a plainclothes officer who impatiently took down some notes. We listened in.

Professor Obo had checked in at about 10 p.m., alone, and had gone straight to his room. He never came downstairs again and no one asked for him at the desk. There was only one entry to the hotel for guests. The service door outback was used for deliveries and remained closed at all times.

I spotted Ali as he was walking down the staircase into the lobby holding a walkie-talkie in his hand. The Maître d'hôtel stood up quickly as if relieved.

"There is the detective in charge and you can ask him anything. I have told him everything," he said pointing in Ali's direction.

With that he walked briskly to the counter and poured himself a stiff drink.

I could not blame him. This is not the kind of attention one wanted, especially in an industry that relied on reputation. Distraught guests had been asked to stay put while the police conducted a thorough search of the premises. Now that the police had finished their interviews and search, the guests were allowed to leave their rooms and they came streaming down. Some came to check out and demanded full refunds while others just walked to the curb to get a taxi.

"What the fuck is going on, boy?" asked one very irate tourist, his duffel bag in one hand and holding a cigar in the other.

I looked up, wondering why a father would talk to his son that way and realised that he was talking to the manager.

"Nothing, sir, it's really nothing," the manager pleaded, holding out his hands as if trying to stop him from leaving.

"You haven't heard the last of this!" the white tourist shouted back, at him, staring him down.

"Sir, it's just a dead African. The police are here investigating. You are safe here, *hakuna matata*."

The tourist walked off in a huff, leaving the manager humiliated and lost. Many of the other tourists, however, on finding out that it was not a tourist who had been found dead, continued with their itineraries. It had been a busy agonising morning for everyone and the guests seemed relieved to get on with their lives having, in their view, narrowly escaped murder. That was the mayhem at Hotel Waldoria. Otieno and I were about to confront the manager when I saw Ali walking across the lobby.

"Ali!" I called out.

He turned to look at me for a second, gave some commands on the walkie-talkie and walked towards us.

"Well, well, well. If it's not the writers!" he said with a playful smile.

"I am beginning to suspect you two - showing up at every crime scene!"

"Anything you can tell us?" I asked.

"Stay away from my crime scene!" he said and then smiled a little.

As we walked outside, Ali Fana gave us the rundown. The death was exactly like the others except this time a guest in an adjacent room, a tourist from Finland, thought she had heard some commotion, and what she thought was the voice of a woman. On further questioning, she said that she and her African lover, a man she had met at the bar, had been a little pre-occupied and a little inebriated so she was not quite sure. Her lover on the other hand had heard nothing.

The police were in the process of reviewing the closed circuit cameras in the hotel lobby to see if there was an unregistered guest, man or woman, who had walked into the hotel within the last twenty four hours - or any person that might be of interest.

"Ali, with all these killings, has there been any ransom notes found anywhere, in emails, phone records that might indicate extortion?" I asked him somberly.

"We have checked all the emails, phone records, and personal contacts of the three victims looking for a common thread. Nothing has really stood out; and there are no ransom notes. We have nothing to tie all three murders together except for the similarity of the *MO*. But tell you what, and you can quote me on it: I think we are ready to declare this the work of a serial killer!"

With that he excused himself and walked off to talk with the Inspector.

I had not heard from Irene just yet but this new development had thrown a damper on that theory about Abscor. I would still follow up on it but Ali Fana was right; there was a serial killer on the loose. It was the only conclusion that made sense. And I ran with the story.

* * *

Several hours later, *The Daily Grind* ran a special edition, which was gobbled up within the minutes of its hitting the stands. The TV crews and radio stations ran their breaking news shortly afterwards. They all followed my lead.

The city of Nairobi almost came to a standstill. Everyone was talking about it and speculation was rife. Talk of strange men harvesting human parts for sale to American markets was supplanted by other equally outrageous rumours. For a few days, even sex workers were said to have refused to do business with tourists, which prompted the tourist board to issue a statement denying that any such harvest had taken place in a major hotel.

One thing was for sure: No one knew when, how or why the serial killer would strike - or whom!

Men started going home early and bars, whose patronage usually swelled after office hours, began to close earlier for lack of customers. It was rumoured that some wives were elated to finally have their husbands and the fathers of their children home to eat dinner with them without reeking of alcohol, cigarettes and old farts. Others did not care too much one way or the other - life had to go on.

Later that evening, Ali Fana, the lead detective in this case, flanked by the Commissioner of Police, appeared on national TV to assure the nation that his team was on track to catch the serial killer. He looked and sounded the part of a confident sleuth about to nab the perpetrator. He became a national figure. I, on the other hand, was the first to give the killings a name that caught fire: *City Murders!*

CHAPTER NINE

● ● ● · · ● ● ●

Although I was glad to have broken the story and the formulation that was being used by all media stations, I knew nothing had really been solved. But I was determined to get to the bottom of it, and as soon as Ali had made an arrest, I wanted to be the first one on it and the one source with all the details. That meant that I had to keep at it, digging deeper into any and all possible leads. Although Ali kept me updated, officially of course, I needed more than he was giving - one had to rely on the brow of one's sweat as well.

I had promised Irene that I would dig up information on Abscor but I was not getting anywhere with that angle except for confirmation from Ali that it was indeed true that Abscor's representatives had come into the country for consultations with KEMRI. What was not true was the talk of a possible merger with a local pharmaceutical company. He told me that KenPharm had folded almost five years ago - we had checked it out as well and found that they had long closed shop.

I sought and met with Professor Obo's wife one late evening at their home in Kileleshwa. She was obviously very upset but I assured her that my reporting would only help bring the serial killer or killers to justice. She had nothing to add to what she had already told the lead detective, she told me. She would be going to see him later on in the week for updates.

"I know him personally - Detective Ali - he's a fine investigator," I said to reassure her.

She looked haggard, almost defeated, and I did not want to take too much of her time. But we talked for a bit.

"Mrs. Obo, did your husband know Dr. Kizito or collaborated on anything with KEMRI?"

I knew it was a long shot but like Ali had said, use the process of elimination. She looked puzzled. Her lips quivered as if she was trying to find something to say. I could see her mind was racing and I sought to quieten any unpleasant thoughts I might have inadvertently brought upon her.

"Let me clarify that," I hastened to say. "I'm trying to see how all these murders connect, if they do. I know the police are working hard on the cases. My detective friend tells me that publicity is a necessary part of police investigations. Someone somewhere saw or heard something and the publicity might encourage them to come forward. So if there is anything you can tell me, anything at all, please do not hesitate."

"There is really nothing that I can think of," she said, shaking her head, firmly.

"Was your husband seeing anyone at all?" I asked but the question came out wrong.

"I don't like your insinuation. My husband would not hide anything from me."

"I did not mean that he was doing anything illegal. It's just that it does not make sense for someone who is so well respected to be found in a hotel without …"

"Do not even go there! My husband was not like that. I think you better leave," she said and stood up. "Please, just leave!"

I stood up, reached into my jacket for a business card and handed it to her. She did not take it.

I did not feel like going back to the office. I called Otieno and Mburu but they were not available for a drink, but I suspected that they had succumbed to the terror of the serial killer. Nonetheless, I passed by the London Grill to see Meredith.

Nightfall was fast approaching so I was not going to stay long. I sat quietly in a corner and ordered my usual, *Irio* and a cold tusker. Though Meredith was on duty, she was busy and I was not seeing much of her, so after I polished my plate, I headed out to the bus station.

That evening the bus came sooner than I had anticipated so I choked off the tip of my cigarette with my thumb and index finger as

I hopped in. The little firecracker burnt a little but I was not about to waste a whole stick on account of a bus. So I stomped the cinder and put the remainder of the cigarette in my pocket.

I sat by the window next to a neatly dressed lady who had to make way for me by moving her legs to one side while I squeezed by. She adjusted her skirt and then she placed a huge purse across her thighs as if to hide them from roving eyes. Without saying a word, I pulled myself closer and leaned my head against the window pane, watching the city rush behind us.

I must have dozed off because the next thing I remember was the bus conductor shaking me violently to wake me up. We had come to the last stop at Dagoretti and everyone had alighted except for me. I looked around quickly, trying to get my bearings. I paid up and then stepped out into the night, thanking the conductor who just looked at me as he muttered something about old people. I was not any older than he was but I let it go.

After taking a few steps towards my apartment, I stopped to re-light my crooked stump of a cigarette. I was not interested in looks, just some rotten nicotine. The pungent smell of stale tobacco hit my nostrils and the sulfur dioxide from the match made me cough violently but I composed myself. For the umpteenth time, I promised myself to cut down on smoking - soon!

It had gotten colder now and so I walked briskly, trying to stay warm. I had not made more than fifteen steps when a shadowy figure appeared in front of me. It was not very dark but I could not make out who it was. The thought crept into my mind - the serial killer. I felt myself tense up, my heart beating faster. I thought about running back towards the bus stop - surely there would be people by the kiosk. I could see my apartment just straight ahead but it now looked distant, unreachable and almost foreign.

I controlled myself through an odd mixture of curiosity and pride. It made sense that the serial killer should come after the person who had written the story for *The Daily Grind*. A soft cough made me glance quickly behind me. There was another shadowy figure fast approaching me. Alarmed, I threw down my cigarette and took my left hand out of my pocket but continued walking, hoping for the best. I tried to convince myself that I was overreacting but I knew what I was feeling was real. I had to make a decision quickly but I felt paralysed. I had nowhere to run.

I took a deep breath and let it out slowly, trying to quieten my nerves. I looked behind me. The shadowy figure was right upon me, so I stepped aside to let him pass by, watching him very closely.

Just when he got in front of me, he turned quickly to face me, suddenly throwing a wild right cross to my face. I ducked to my left and quickly came up with a left hook to the body and followed it with a right upper cut that caught him in the jaw, snapping his head back. He obviously had not expected this and frankly, neither had I. He spun out and lunged at me with his outstretched arms. I instinctively kicked him before tackling him to the ground and pinning him under me. I peppered his head with lefts, rights and elbows all the while yelling obscenities. I was hoping someone would hear the commotion and come to my aid.

I felt someone grab me from behind, fumbling to get a good grip on my neck. I was still throwing blow after blow in blind rage at the mugger pinned under me. He wiggled this way and that way trying to avoid the punishment but I was not about to let him go. Suddenly, the fucker on my neck gave up and started hammering my head with his fists.

I grabbed his right hand with my left and pulled him violently towards me. He stumbled forward but maintained his balance and tried to push me off his friend. I pulled myself up and slapped him hard. His friend writhed from under me and just as he was about to get on his feet, I drove down an elbow right to his nose. He fell down holding his face with both hands for protection. I jumped on him.

"You bloody bastard!" I yelled.

He started begging, "G-g-get him off of m-m-me!"

His voice had a register of fear and I knew he was about done. I lifted my right elbow high and, putting all my body weight behind it, I drove it right into is face. Crack! I felt that unmistakable crunch of his nose giving way. He screamed in pain and started crying loudly and pleading for me not to hit him again.

"You b-b-broke my n-n-nose!"

I drove my elbow one more time to his face. He made a grunting sound and I knew he was done.

His friend was not having any luck placing a choke-hold on my neck. He gave up and pushed his stocky little fingers in my face, trying to hook them into my nostrils. I jerked my head backwards and butted him right in his mouth. His teeth tore into my scalp and I felt a warm trickle down my neck. He grabbed my left arm and begun punching the top of my head again. He then yanked me hard to the right and I fell off. I used that momentum to get to my feet. I turned around quickly and punched him with a left-right combination that pushed him back. I was getting ready to pounce with a flying kick but I tripped and fell forward.

The stocky fellow landed a blow to the back of my head as I fell flat on my face. I rolled over and lay on my back trying to attack from a crouched position. They both stood over me, kicking wildly at my legs and ribs. I lay on my back trying to thwart the attack. I knew that I could not take both of them at once but the short dude was done and I knew if I hit him one more time I could knock his ass out. With everything I had left in me, I quickly got to my feet and rushed towards him, grunting and landed two blows to the body - the 'animal' was loose! I followed with an upper cut.

He had had enough. He turned to run but I tackled from behind and brought him to his knees. I punched him in the gut as we came to the ground. I tried to flip him over but he slipped off my grip and ran away into the darkness. I turned to face his accomplice, who, after mulling over his options, decided to flee in the opposite direction.

Just then I heard a car engine start and I turned towards the bus stop just as the headlights came on. I heard the engine rev and the car then sped off.

The adrenaline in my system began to wear off. I hurried home and locked the door behind me. My sides felt like they were on fire from the kicks I had absorbed. Still gasping for air, I went to the mirror and looked myself over. Apart from the gush on my scalp, I had suffered no major injury - no broken bones or serious cuts. I placed an icepack on a wash cloth and pushed it against my scalp to stop the bleeding.

I grabbed the phone and dialed Ali's number. It rang a few times before I hung up. What did I expect him to do? I thought of calling the local police but I knew that they would take hours to come. I felt some comfort knowing that the thugs might not come back to finish what they had started - I had severely hurt one of them and I also lived in an apartment complex. I had neighbours. They could jump me on the way but they would not dare attack me at home – at least not tonight.

I was quite shaken and did not fall asleep until the wee hours of morning.

*   *   *

I woke up late the next morning in a world of pain. I reached into the small drawer on my night stand and pulled out a packet of aspirin. I threw my head back as I swallowed three, chased them down with a glass of water and walked gingerly to the shower. A nice hot shower would do the trick, I hoped.

After breakfast, I called Otieno and relayed the news of my attack. He was alarmed and advised me to call Ali immediately, which I did. Ali came to the phone promptly. I quickly told him that I had been attacked the previous night but I was okay. He was shocked but at once dismissed my theory of a pair of serial killers. The attack did not fit the previous pattern. He asked me if I had taken a good look at the getaway car and if I had the number plates. I said no, it was dark. He asked me for other details. I told him that they did not have any weapons and they had not even asked me to give up my wallet or anything, they had just pounced on me.

"I don't think you need to read too much into it," he said. "It could be just a mugging, my friend, you know how it is. I'm glad you are okay though."

"Something doesn't quite add up, man. I'm beginning to think that I was set up. It was like they were either waiting for or following me."

"Come on, man. Druggies wait for anyone so they can get some money for a fix."

"But that's the thing, they did not even…"

"Chidi, just don't worry. I will have someone look into it. Just be careful," he added.

"I will be," I answered, more to myself than to Ali.

I was about to hang up when Ali, his voice raised in agitation asked me if I could make it in town inside the hour.

"Why, what's up man?"

"Our killer has struck again."

CHAPTER TEN

Ali and I arrived at the River Road Motel together. John Solstice Wakaba, the latest victim, was found here naked, his clothes neatly folded, resting on the corner of the night stand together with his wedding ring. He was still holding a sealed condom in his hand. Except for the wallet and some loose change strewn on the floor, there was no other indication of foul play. As Ali took command, I stayed close, watching and listening.

So far these murders did not fit anything I had ever seen or read about. How was it that the victims seemed to be going to their deaths willingly? Or were their bodies being staged - someone's sick sexual fantasies? But even that did not make sense. The question still remained: how? In the movies, the bad guys always left something behind by which they were later caught - but not in any of these cases.

Ali looked puzzled, as were the other detectives. Like the cases before this, there was no forced entry, no physical trauma, no murder weapon or any signs of struggle. How was the killer or killers able to do it without leaving any trace evidence? Were the crime scenes being staged? Whoever they were, they were good. That meant that they could get to anyone if and when they wanted. The danger was palpable and looking at Ali, I knew that he was under immense pressure - the country was going nuts!

"We got to get this guy, people," Ali said addressing his team. "Run this place down, every inch. I want to know who the fuck is doing this. Give me something!"

One officer came running up to Ali. He seemed excited about something and I inched closer. It turned out that the first uniforms responding to the scene had uncovered surveillance footage from a security camera in the lobby. Ali was beside himself with excitement. A break in the case!

"Did anyone look at the tape?" he asked.

Yes, they had viewed the tape and in it they were able to make out a man, later identified as Wakaba, walking into the motel closely followed by what appeared to be a man in a trench coat pushing a shopping cart. It turned out, after combing through the evidence that the man pushing the cart was none other than Wagateru, as identified by the motel manager. He was a well-known street hawker and a frequent visitor to the motel. The police were on the way to pick him up.

Ali was ecstatic. "Excellent work, corporal, excellent work. Let me know as soon as they have him in custody." He looked at me and smiled.

After a half-hour or so, Ali's phone rang. He spun around and pulled out his cell phone. I could not make out what was being said but according to Ali's responses, it sounded serious. They had Wagateru in custody. He was being held at the Central Police Station. Ali wanted to interrogate him right away but he was having problems with jurisdiction.

"I am the lead detective!" he yelled over the phone.

After a brief conversation, Ali told the other side that he would be there first thing in the morning. It was hard dealing with bureaucracy - even for a detective.

I decided that this was the best time to head out on my own. So I excused myself and left.

I went to the Central Police Station and asked to speak with the Officer in Charge. The constable at the desk asked me to wait while he disappeared into a room marked OCPD. I could hear hushed admonitions about getting the press off their backs before he came back, smiled and asked me to step right in.

I found the officer sitting with her hands clasped together on top of her desk. I introduced myself and she asked me to take a seat. It was one of those wooden chairs that had seen a lot of use through the years and was in need of some repair. I sat down, pulled out my note pad and fumbled for my pen.

"You are the one who wrote that story about the so-called City Murders. What can I do for you Mr. Chide?" she asked.

"Chidi" I corrected her, hoping that her recognising my name would yield good things. "Tell me, can you confirm that you have arrested someone in relation to the murder of Wakaba?"

"I will neither confirm nor deny. But we have arrested many people and they will all be arraigned in the courts," she said, smiling.

"I am particularly interested in Wagateru. Can you tell me why you are holding him?"

She did not respond but just smiled and looked at me.

"Could you at least tell me on what grounds you have arrested him?"

She quickly straightened up, cleared her throat: they were under orders not to disclose the nature of any ongoing investigation. She opened the door and held it open, marking the end of our conversation.

I left and headed to my office.

* * *

The next morning I learned that Wagateru had been released and that no charges would be pressed against him. I called Ali, hoping that he would give me something to write about. The investigation was back to square one. Ali was not a happy camper, going by his tone on the phone, when I asked him about Wagateru.

"The son-of-a-bitch had nothing for us," he thundered. "He kept repeating some incoherent bullshit about fruits and a woman he was supposed to meet."

I let Ali vent his frustrations then asked him whether I could see the video tape.

"Why do you want the tape?" he asked, in a calmer voice, a good sign.

"Perhaps there is something there that I can write about."

He was quiet for a minute, contemplating my request, I guessed.

"Can you get me the tape?" I repeated.

"No, man, you know I can't do that. Police evidence, Jack, but I'll let you know if we have any new developments."

He was right but it never hurts to try. I was a little disappointed but that was the business I was in. You knocked on as many doors as you could. Sooner or later one of them would open.

"Ok, man. Just a heads up: I'll try and talk to Wagateru," I said on the spur of the moment. "Perhaps he can tell me something he did not feel comfortable telling the police."

I heard Ali chuckle but he knew I had a point. Most people feared the police and, worse still, no one wanted to be called a snitch. It was us against them - criminals and law-abiding citizens alike against the enforcers of the law that was supposed to protect all.

"Good luck man, I interviewed him myself and got nothing. What makes you think he will tell you any different?"

Despite the chuckle, his voice sounded hurt. I knew that I had overstepped my boundaries by implying I could do a better job of it but that was not what I meant. I needed to be more sensitive to people's feelings. I had to work on having to think before I opened my mouth - people could get hurt by loose lips.

"Ah, come on, man, you know what I mean," I pleaded.

"It's ok, Jack. Just make sure you touch base with me after you talk to him so we can compare notes. That has been our understanding since you came to me for help, remember?"

I read sincerity in his voice.

"Yeah, man. I got you, but it cuts both ways."

I remembered something he had told me a long time back: when one hand washes the other, they both become clean. He needed to start scrubbing - I was running out of angles and I needed this story.

CHAPTER ELEVEN

A few days passed without any development in the investigations, except for the police offer of a substantial reward for any information leading to an arrest of the serial killer.

Other bulletins were advisories to the hospitality industry urging them to update their security measures - video surveillance, watchmen and proper logging of all guests. The public was asked to be vigilant but not alarmed. I felt that far from reassuring the nation, these announcements were an admission that the police investigations had stalled.

I decided to seek out Wagateru so I walked over to River Road. I had to wiggle through what seemed to be thousands of people buying, selling and haggling over the prices of goods; beds, TVs, jewelry, car batteries and foods including roasted corn on the cob. I made it to the corner of Luthuli Avenue and River Road where I had been told Wagateru spent his days selling vegetables and candy from a make-shift pushcart. He was not there today.

A woman, her mangoes displayed on a sack and piled up into a triangle, called out to me:

"Hey, get three mangoes for twenty shillings, special offer!"

I walked over to her. She kept on waving off some flies that nestled on the mangoes, they would fly and land on some other pile, and the struggle would continue.

"I'll take two for ten," I bent over and sat on my heels.

"Three for twenty, these are imported, not the regular ones you find all over the place," she said, throwing her hands dismissively at the local fruit.

"Well, okay, I will take the three," I decided not to haggle, handing her a twenty shilling note.

"Can I peel one for you, eh? Very juicy!" she said as she quickly folded the note and placed it inside her bra, thus sealing the transaction.

She picked out three mangoes and put them in a Bata shoe plastic bag and handed them to me.

"Say, do you know the man who sells wares over there?" I asked pointing to Wagateru's cart.

She gave me a once over, deciding whether to trust me or not. I pulled out another twenty and gave it to her. She took the twenty and looked at me, expectantly. I placed another twenty in her hand.

"Who are you looking for exactly?" she asked after she had secured the bills inside her bra.

"Wagateru, that's his name," I answered.

"He has not been here for…let me see," she looked up into the air trying to remember the last time she had seen him. "Oh, well, he came back after he was released and then some people came for him again."

"Who came for him?" I asked, alarmed and confused.

"I don't know but they looked like business people, you know the ones with suits and all."

"When was this?"

"It could have been the day before yesterday, or the one before, I don't know. Maybe three days. They grabbed him right there and put him inside a car and drove off."

"Do you know what kind of car they…"

"No," she answered quickly and started tending to another customer who had stopped to buy some mangoes.

I left. Something did not quite add up. Why would the police release him and then turn around and arrest him again? It had to be someone else but whom? I called Ali. We agreed to meet at the Jeevanjee Gardens within the hour.

I went back to the office to check my email and then headed out to meet Ali who was waiting for me by the entrance.

"If it's not the scribe himself," Ali said in greeting.

I shook his hand and tightened my grip playfully. He winced but as I eased up on my grip, he pulled his hand out and without warning, grabbed my fingers and squeezed hard. The pain shot up my hand forcing me down to my knees.

"Alright ... alright! I get it."

He let go and helped me up. We sat on a nearby bench right by the entrance. It was a nice day to be out, I thought, as I looked around. There were not that many people milling around the park just yet. By lunch time, it would be packed to capacity. The trees and shrubs gave a natural colour to the city of concrete and glass.

"How have you been?" I asked after we had both lit up.

He pulled on his cigarette and let the smoke drift out slowly.

"We are doing okay, I guess."

He shrugged his shoulders and smiled, which told me that he was in a better mood so I went straight to the subject of Wagateru. It was always easy to get answers when he was like this but first, he wanted to hear what I had to say. So I narrated my visit with the mango lady. She had seen him being picked up by men in suits. I knew how that sounded but that's all I had.

"Who told you this again?" he asked cheekily. He then let out a small chuckle.

I knew where he was going with this but why would a street hawker make up such a story? I did not answer him so he continued.

"Nobody has reported his disappearance, and I can't see why my men would arrest him again."

I asked him if he could at least look into it.

"Why are you suddenly interested in the street hawker?"

"Man, I'm just looking for a story. You know how it is."

"I will definitely look into it," he assured me.

"So what do you guys have on the murders, unofficially of course?" I asked, taking advantage of the mood.

Ali had formulated a profile of the perpetrator of the city murders, based on what he called "the facts." The fact, for instance, that all the victims were found in hotels not too far from their homes meant they were mostly family men. The fact that they had rented the rooms for the night suggested that women were involved. The fact that there was no forced entry, no murder weapon and that the method of killing was undetectable or as yet undetermined, suggested a certain amount of professionalism, perhaps a hit man. He concluded that this was the work of a loner who, for some unknown reason, had a disdain for wealth.

I did not tell him but I was a little disappointed by his fact-based profile of the killer. The profile or profiles did nothing to narrow the field of would-be suspects. It could have been anyone. I did not know if he was telling me this so I could run a piece in the paper or whether he was just thinking out loud, trying to convince himself that he was making progress where there was none.

I felt sorry for him. It was as plain as day that the police had nothing to work with, and the Coroner's office was no help. Perhaps they needed outside input but I dared not say this - I had already pricked at his pride with my insinuation that I could extract information from Wagateru where he had failed.

"It is true that all murders have a common theme," I said, agreeing with him, more out of pity than conviction, but he had said nothing that I could use as a story.

I thought of something to say to help us focus on the missing parts; his face had lost its earlier vivacity: it had that tired look one gets from lack of sleep. It was clear that the top brass was breathing heavily on his neck to solve these crimes and the pressure was getting to him. He was usually quite an engaging character with an easy manner about him, but lately, his demeanor had changed - he looked forlorn. With no leads to follow, he was just like me - grabbing at straws. Perhaps it was time to call in Scotland Yard, the FBI or the Israelis - it would not be the first time.

"Hey, so what happens now?" I asked Ali after a little awkward silence.

"Here, let me buy you a drink," he said, pointing to a quiet little bar off Biashara Street.

It sounded like a good idea. We crossed the busy street and entered Garden City bar. He called Otieno and asked him to join us there. After a brief moment, I called Mburu - we might as well have some fun.

Not much activity here except for a few revelers enjoying their favourites drinks. We ordered two cold Tuskers. The waiter brought the drinks and I offered him the imported mangoes. He looked at me, confused at my generosity but made off with the bag. He mumbled something about produce replacing tips but I did not pay him too much mind.

"What happens now with the investigations?" I asked again.

Ali shrugged his shoulders resignedly this time.

"I must tell you, this is puzzling," he lamented. "I am trying to find the common threads in these murders, a pattern or signature if you will. Every serial killer has a signature. But I can't find one here, just a goddamn theme."

"But what does your gut tell you?"

"My guess is that this could also be the work of a very sophisticated gang that is luring these men to motels using women as bait. But what I find intriguing is the manner of death. The Coroner's office has not been able to make a determination as to the cause of death. I find this very puzzling - and I am getting a little impatient. I mean, what do they do all day? I need to know what is killing these buggers. The sooner they get me something, the sooner I can apprehend the perpetrator. Right now, it feels like we are just waiting for the killer to make a mistake. But I take it as a challenge…the only problem is that people are dying!"

I wished there was something I could do to help him and in a sense help myself. Perhaps if I got him to talk more about the murders, it might trigger something they were overlooking. So I began to pry into how they were conducting the investigation, exactly what they were looking for at the crime scene, but he continued with his varying profiles of the killer or killers. It was as though he was talking to himself so I just listened - trying to glean something that might be newsworthy.

I sipped on my drink and pulled out a cigarette. I was about to light it when something Ali had said suddenly registered: that the Coroner's Department had not been able to ascertain the cause of death. I do not know why I had not thought of this before but the Coroner must have their suspicions. I could use that for my story! Of course I would have to cite "unofficial sources."

Ali and I were becoming more like each other. Like him, my mind was just reaching for anything, any piece of information that might begin to make sense of it all. I was also, like him, trying this and that - you just never knew how, where or when your case or story would find legs and so you just kept at it, digging and scraping until it revealed itself. But where I was looking for a story, he was looking for the killer.

Ali pulled the cigarette dangling from my fingers and lit it up. I had not known him to smoke this much.

"Man, you need to get some rest," I offered.

He really looked like he had aged considerably these last few weeks.

"Tell me about it," he said, almost gratefully.

I seized the opportunity.

"Hey, Ali, since I cannot find Wagateru, do you think you can get me that video?"

"What video?" he asked noisily, fumbling through his pockets for something.

"Oh, the one with Wagateru and Wakaba" I answered quickly, as if it was not a big deal.

"Man, I told you, and you know it, I cannot give you police evidence, come on!"

"But you can describe what's in it, the details?"

"There was really nothing in it," he said matter-of-factly. "But between you and me, I can tell you that it's just a waste of time. You do get to see Wakaba and Wagateru, some prostitutes but nothing tangible. We have questioned those we could find but nothing came out of that."

Well, it was worth a try. So I laid the matter to rest.

It was slightly after four o'clock. It was early but I needed to get home before dark. I did not want to be out late for fear that I might be attacked again. My attackers did not fit any of the profiles Ali had drawn but the fact remained that they had attacked me - next time they might bring a gun.

I looked at Ali and was about to bring up the subject of my attack, then decided against it. He had not brought it up all day and I did not want to appear weak, shaken or too concerned. Still, since the attack, I shuddered at the thought of being alone in my apartment. I could have gone to my mother's house but I was not sure I could stand her barrage of questions. My masculinity had to remain intact.

We sat there for a while, sipping our drinks quietly, but I knew that our minds were in the same place, looking for different things from the same site. It was in times like this that I missed Otieno. I wondered why it was taking him so long to meet us. It was unlike him to be late for an afternoon drink but I gathered he was tying up his weekly column. One cannot be blamed for putting in an honest day's work.

Ali was about to leave when Otieno and Mburu came bustling through the door. Otieno was wearing his usual brown corduroy jacket, a worker's jacket, as he called it. He sat next to me in the booth and excitedly ordered a cold Tusker Premium while Mburu sat on the opposite side. Mburu ordered a soda, lamenting that he had to work early the next morning. He was very well-disciplined when it came to his drinking and his work but that did not stop him from looking at my beer longingly.

"Why did you all decide to meet here, of all places?" Mburu asked, looking around disapprovingly.

"It was Ali's idea," I said loudly, pointing at him. "You all know how he likes these seedy joints."

I smiled at Ali mockingly. He was about to respond but nothing came quickly and the moment passed. Mburu looked around again and mockingly muttered under his breath, cursing the stars above and the people who worshipped the moon. We all broke out in laughter - it was not that bad a joint to begin with and the beer was cheaper than at the Grill.

"Hey, Jack, did that lady call you back?" Otieno asked after the laughter subsided.

That piqued Ali's interest and so he pulled his jacket over his shoulders and leaned forward.

"Oh, you talked to Meredith already, you devil you! Why didn't you tell me?"

He was smiling, waiting to hear the juicy details of my Meredith. But before I could get a word in, Otieno interjected, almost standing from his seat.

"No, he was going to see Professor Obo's wife, what's her name, the one at the University?"

Otieno was looking up in the ceiling, trying to remember her name.

I sipped on my beer, waiting for Ali's reaction any minute now. He turned his gaze at me, then to Otieno and finally back to me, puzzled.

"You did not tell me you had spoken to her. When did you see her?"

Then he sat down, placing his jacket on his lap. His face looked a little terse, betrayed sort of, but I had done nothing wrong, I told myself. We were both in this - just in different capacities.

"I went to visit her the other day…." I started. I did not feel like I needed to justify myself to anyone, least of all to Ali. I was doing my job.

"I thought we agreed to share information?" Ali asked with a hint of irritation.

"Yes, when there's information to share," I said.

"I don't think you should be investigating crimes which are under police investigation without some coordination with us. You may interfere with the process without your knowing it."

"Dude, I am a reporter. This is what we do. We ask questions."

"We agreed to share. You've been holding out on me, Jack?"

"Listen. All I asked her to do was find out if her husband knew Dr. Kizito and whether they had collaborated on any project," I explained, trying to lower the temperature.

He looked at me for a minute then said, "I can't believe you, man. All afternoon and you had something but did not share."

He had that hurt look again and I felt bad for the man but I did not see what the big deal was. He was overreacting. I hoped someone would jump in this to ease the tension and I was more than happy when Mburu joined in.

"You guys sound like you have some unresolved issues, some beef, as we say in the streets." He looked at me, then at Ali and gestured that we should shake hands.

"There's no beef. Everyone is just on edge."

I turned to Ali, who was tense, to shake hands but he ignored me.

"You know what Professor Abo's wife told me?" I asked rhetorically.

"What did she say?" he asked, resignedly - like what was he going to do?

"Nothing - she actually took exception to my saying that her husband had been in a motel. She thought I was implying he was cheating on her. She asked me to leave. She did not even take my business card. Obviously, this is not something I want to shout from rooftops. I have some dignity…"

I felt myself getting upset but I held on. For some reason, they all burst out laughing. The atmosphere relaxed.

"Women seem to like jilting you," Otieno said, grinning widely.

He had set himself up so I went for it.

"Dude, your wife *Otieno-ed* the hell out of your behind, so if I were you, I would not be speaking at all."

The image of Akinyi running after Otieno with a broom was just too much and everyone burst out laughing again. The thunderous laughter soon tapered off just as the juke box came alive with Kalamashaka - a local music group with some real groovy beats.

"On that note, I am out," Mburu said. "I have an early morning. But Jack, from tomorrow I have several days of vacation and I'm ready to party! Do you mind if I come up to Dago?"

"No, man! Come on up, any time after five."

Mburu left.

It would be nice to just hang out with Mburu and catch up on family, I thought to myself. I needed a break, to just chill out and not think about work and all these killings. It would also be a relief to have company with me in my apartment - safety in numbers.

Even before the attack on me, I had been feeling like I was being followed or like I was being watched. I had received phone calls where the caller would just hang up. But these did not register as evil intents. In the office, we received many of these calls from informants and whistle blowers who would change their minds on hearing that "hello." Others came from people our reports and investigative pieces had offended. I had never really felt like I was exposed, like I was naked and I always chalked it off as being overly cautious or just a hint of what I so eloquently called anticipatory anxiety.

"Alright, gang. I'm out too - trying to catch the kids before they sleep," Ali said as he picked up his jacket again and the bill and went to the bar counter to pay up.

After a little while he came back to the table. He shook our hands and said he was probably just tired and needed to get home to rest, his way of apologising for the tension. I told him I would get in touch with him the next day. He mumbled something and then walked out.

"I don't see what the big deal was," Otieno said after a while.

"Don't blame our friend. He must be under intense pressure to stop this murderer. I cannot begin to imagine what that is like," I said.

Otieno was silent for a minute and then shook his head.

"You may be right but I have known Ali longer than you. I don't think he ever forgave you for screwing his sister. That's why these flare-ups occur from time to time."

I looked at him expecting to see that familiar grin but it was not there.

"There is nothing I can do about the past, man. I liked the girl," I said as I looked around the bar helplessly.

The place was packing up quickly and darkness would be creeping in before long. "We better head out soon," I said to Otieno who walked over to sit on the other side of the table facing me. He pulled his drink towards him and took a long swig.

"I know you are a little shaken up from the other day," he said, letting out a long loud belch. "If you want, you can come and stay with us for a while."

The grin was back.

He said this almost halfheartedly but I gave it a serious consideration. It was not a bad idea but it was one I could not accept, at least not just yet. I would have to go home at some point or keep running forever.

We sipped on our beers in silence for a while.

"Did you make anything of the car that took off that night?" Otieno asked after ordering another round of drinks.

"No, but it was as if whoever was in it was watching me," I reflected.

"You know it could just be some local thugs who jumped at a chance to get some quick cash. Or it could be that someone really does not like the fact that you are poking around."

It had occurred to me that it was possible that I was just another victim of a crime infested city and its suburbs but for some reason that made me feel worse. I know it sounded ridiculous but by some demented logic, it felt like there was some dignity in being purposefully targeted than just being a random victim. I kept that thought to myself, knowing Otieno would crucify me if he heard of it.

The waiter brought the drinks and popped them open. At this rate, I would never get home early but I was not about to complain. I could always get a cab to drop me off right at the gate to my apartment complex, I reasoned, knowing very well that it was not going to happen that way. But it worked to soothe that part of me that was being cautious.

After about an hour, and a succulent piece of chicken with a side dish of French fries, we finally caught the bus and headed home.

"Would you want me to walk you home?" Otieno asked facetiously.

"Don't make me rearrange your face or worse, hurt you, man," I teased him. "Akinyi will really throw your ass out for ugliness."

"Just holler if you hear something," he answered and with that he walked off towards his house.

I peered hard into darkness as I started down the dusty road to my apartment. I could feel my heart beating hard against my chest. I should not have had that last beer, I said to myself as I shook the cobwebs from my head. I really needed to get a handle on this drinking bullshit.

When I got to my door, I fumbled for the key and just as I was about to get it into the lock, I felt something brush against my hands.

I jumped back and that's when I noticed that it was a noose hanging from the hinge! I turned around quickly to look behind me. There was no one there. I looked at the noose again and that's when I saw what appeared to be a piece of paper sticking out at the bottom of the door. I picked it up and then, as quietly as I could, opened the door and walked in. I turned on the lights and checked all the rooms to make sure there was no one waiting for me. I then sat down and read the note which said:

"We are watching you. Try on this tie before you die."

There was a drawing of a stick-man hanging from a tree. That is when panic set in. I grabbed my phone and called the police.

After I finished my report the dispatcher said that since it was not an emergency they would send someone in the morning. For now, she advised me to lock the doors and windows and get some rest.

I had hardly sat on the couch to work out my next move - whether I should sleep here or not, when the phone rang. I jumped up in fear: at this hour? Somebody must have been following me. Or they wanted to confirm that I was home. I remembered I had just called the police and perhaps they were sending someone right away. I picked up the phone hoping the dispatcher had decided to send officers after all.

"Hi! Is this Chidi?" a woman's voice asked.

"Yes. Who are you?" I asked, trying to tone down any aggression.

"It's Irene. Dr. Kiz..."

"Yes, yes, Irene, so good to hear from you," I said with great relief, then guilt since I had no news to offer her - but I was still working the case and that's all that mattered. "How are you doing?"

"I'm doing okay," she answered. "I found something that may or may not be of interest. I checked my brother's bank statements."

"Go on!" I urged her when she paused.

I could hear some paper rustling and then she continued.

"There is nothing here that shows deposits from Abscor or any pharmaceuticals."

She paused again.

Damn! We were back to square one. I felt deflated.

"Oh, well. I'm sure we will get to the bottom of it," I said, trying to reassure her but I did not even believe that myself.

"No, wait, ah, here it is….this is why I called you."

I sat up and pressed the phone to my ear, my heart was pounding with anticipation.

"No, it's just a withdrawal but it is quite a hefty sum.....hmmm, this is strange."

"What is it?"

"It looks like my brother had withdrawn a large sum of money the day of his murder." She sounded puzzled and her voice trailed off.

"How much was it and where?" I asked.

"This is crazy…thousands, withdrawn from… er… let me see …" she paused as if trying to make out the wording, "…looks like Kimathi Street in Nairobi … and a check image, for a quarter of a million shillings or something…it says here that it's … made out to a Mr. Kamau Kariuki. The money was withdrawn the next day."

"Holy shit!" I shouted and immediately apologised.

She was quiet for a minute. I did not know what to say either but I knew exactly what this was: this was a deal gone bad or someone was extorting money from him. But why kill him after the fact? Could it have something to do with drugs?

"Do you know him? This Kamau Kariuki?" I asked her, trying to calm my excitement.

No, she did not recall anyone with that name. I thanked her profusely and assured her that I would be in touch with her in the morning. Her phone drove away all thoughts of the noose and the note.

At long last, I had a name of a person who knew Dr. Kizito and who must have had some contact with him before he died. It did not escape my mind that I had also stumbled on the possible motive behind the killings. This was the break I needed. I had done something law enforcement had been unable to do and for a moment, I contemplated going rogue, and breaking the case ahead of the sleuths. But what if I was wrong? The little standoff between Ali and I came back. He had denied me access to the video on professional grounds. I could deny him this information but what exactly could I do with it?

The more I thought about it, the more I was convinced I needed to call Ali. Perhaps with a name, they could track down the killer more quickly than I could, they had the resources anyway. I would still get the story - an exclusive, no less. Although he had admonished me earlier, I knew that I could not possibly sit on this one. This was information that he needed – hell, that we all needed! This was not the time for personal feelings getting in the way of capturing a serial killer. I was in trouble too and the sooner the killer was apprehended, the sooner I would be safe again.

So I dialed Ali's number.

"Hello. Hi, Ali, this is Chidi. I just got a call from Irene," I started, deliberately lowering my voice to hide my excitement, and then it all came out. I told him about the money and about Kamau Kariuki.

After I was done, I waited for him to say something – to show some excitement. This was huge so I was convinced his silence meant well.

"So, what do you think, man? I think we now have this case bagged!" I cajoled.

"Tsk, tsk, tsk. My dear Jack, I really appreciate this but I don't know how to tell you this - we already know about the money and we have an investigator on it as we speak, but thanks all the same," he chided me with a self-assurance that really irked me.

"What? And you didn't tell me?" I said, hardly realising that I had asked him the same question he asked me last night in relation to the professor's wife.

"Jack, there are things I know that I cannot tell you. Perhaps we should talk this face to face so we can come to some understanding about professional boundaries. But don't get me wrong - I will gladly share with you any pertinent information but without impeding the investigation."

"I know what you are saying, man, but you got to throw me something. This is the only story Bulldog will let me work on right now and I really don't have much to go by…that's why I ran this by you."

I felt insulted. What else was he holding out on?

"I appreciate what you are doing. Just let me do the police work - you know that I'm trying to solve a crime and you are trying to write about it. But understand that I appreciate your informing me of your findings."

Cocky bastard! We agreed to meet soon and in our little exchange, I forgot to tell him about the noose and the note.

I lit a cigarette, leaned back on my bed and made smoke rings. He was right, of course. He had a task to do but so did I. On one thing he was wrong - a journalist was not a police informer and I was not going to be his sniffing dog. From now on, he had to give me something first and in return I would share what I had - reciprocity has its place.

CHAPTER TWELVE

●—●—●·●—●—●

I woke up the next morning with a mixture of exhilaration and fear: was I on the verge of solving a case that had perplexed law enforcement? Or was I headed for more trouble? I needed to tie the pieces all together - so much to do and so little time, but I was ready to do whatever it took. The biting chill of an ice-cold shower awoke all my senses and helped me focus on a plan of action. It was going to be a long day, so I wore some comfortable slacks, a T-shirt and sneakers. Then I walked to the bus stop.

Half an hour later, I got off the commuter van named "Destiny's Child" at Kikuyu bus stop. It was too early to call on Irene but I needed to get as much done as I could. I walked up the driveway and entered the compound. I noticed the huge tent that had been erected next to Dr. Kizito's house where some relatives and friends had kept the wake. I could smell the smoke from the smoldering embers by the tent.

I knocked on the door and waited. It was a nice morning but I was feeling apprehensive – kind of antsy.

"Good morning, please do come in," Irene smiled awkwardly as she let me in and into the sitting room. She was wearing a blue gown that made her look more rounded that she was.

She went off to the kitchen and soon came back with some tea and poured two cups, asking me if I wanted some sugar in mine.

"Four sugars, please," I said in jest.

"Oh my God, no ..!" she exclaimed.

"Just kidding," I said, feeling stupid, not because of the poor joke but because of its timing.

But it was good to see her smile nonetheless. I remembered the glint in her eyes when she talked about her family in Texas. So as I sipped my tea, I asked her if she had been in touch with them. Indeed she had, she affirmed with a smile. She looked really nice when her face lit up. She did not offer much else by way of conversation.

"How are you holding up?" I asked, to break the awkward silence.

"One day at a time," she replied. "Sometimes it feels surreal."

I did not know what to say next so I busied myself with my tea. A little while later she pulled a manila folder that was sitting next to her and passed it on to me.

"You will find everything there," she said. "I pulled all his statements for the last three months. I can get more if you want."

Her voice was soft and inclusive. She seemed sweet and kind and I wondered if her husband knew how lucky he was to have her for a wife. I hoped that Meredith and I would work out to be such a couple. I needed a good woman - oh hell, I needed a *woman*!

I finished my tea rather quickly. I was not sure if I should check the records in her presence, so I placed the folder in my bag. I thanked and assured her that I would hold the information confidential and I would let her know as soon as I found something.

Then I stood up and bade her farewell. I walked out slowly but as soon as I was out of sight, I hurried to the bus stop. I could not wait to see what was in the manila folder. Everything seemed to stand still until I finally had the contents in my hands.

I found nothing telling in Dr. Kizito's file: mortgage and credit card payments, gym membership dues, and airline ticket purchases to South Africa, grocery charges and hotel bills, certainly no evidence of financial dealings with Abscor. But Irene was right - two big items stood out: a huge withdrawal on the night of his murder and a check for a quarter of a million shillings made out to and cashed by a Kamau Kariuki a day after the murder. Was the bank withdrawal done before or after his death? I did not know the exact time of Dr. Kizito's death so that would be hard to ascertain. But that did not matter, I still had something.

I had to find this Kamau fellow. He had a lot of questions to answer.

Next, I made it to Wakaba's. His wife made it quite clear that she did not understand why a reporter was interested in this case or why I wanted to publicise what was a family sorrow. I promised her that she would be very interested in what I had to say before she sent me packing.

After my condolences and assurances that I would not write anything injurious or sensational about her family, I told her that I had uncovered huge withdrawals in one of the other victim's bank account at the time of his murder and wondered if she could look into her husband's for any such discrepancies.

She looked at me for a little while and then said, "I don't know if this has any relevance to you but the police have already taken the statement."

"Could you just tell me if there were any large sums withdrawn the day of or after your husband's death?"

"Yes there was. But I think it's best if you ask the police for details."

Although she did not let me ask any more questions, she had at least confirmed a huge withdrawal. Pieces were falling in place - follow the money, it said to me.

Next on the list was a visit to the Kenya Commercial Bank to see my friend Agnes Makau who worked there as an Executive Accounts Manager. I had known her through Linda, my ex-girlfriend and we had remained good friends through the years. What I liked most about her was her easy manner and generous outlook on life. She was always happy, outgoing and ready to jump on the next adventure wherever it presented itself. She was the only person I knew in my circle of friends who had gone sky diving. Perhaps beneath her bravado lay some deep-seated hurt, but she never showed it - there was very little you could say or do to bring her down.

The bank was abuzz with people from all walks of life lined up behind numerous teller stations. Agnes was talking to a young couple when I walked in but a courteous bank representative showed me to a seat and even offered me a cup of coffee while I waited.

"Hey, son, what brings you here?" Agnes said when she was finally able to see me, extending her hand in greeting and wearing that huge smile of hers that I knew so well.

She looked radiant in a beige blouse, grey slacks and matching pumps. I stood up quickly, shook her hand and we walked back to her office.

"You look really nice," I said.

"Yeah, I know," she replied amidst hearty laughter. "You are not so bad yourself."

After a few minutes of banter, I pulled out the bank statement and showed it to her.

"Agnes, I need to get in touch with this guy, Kamau Kariuki."

She perused the document carefully. Then she looked at me like an errant child. The smile was gone. She punched in a code into her computer, and then worked on the keys, squinting to read something on the screen and then keying in some more. Before long, she printed out something and handed it to me without saying a word, an unspoken instruction that I was never to ask her for such another favour again. She then stood up and showed me to the door.

"I think this concludes our business today," she said matter-of-factly.

I shoved the piece of paper in my pocket, shook her hand, thanked her and left.

I walked over to Jason's Kitchen, a small dive that specialised in chicken and waffles. I sat in a corner and ordered half a chicken and a coke. I had everything I needed but I was not going to confront Kamau alone. I called Otieno to meet me at the Khoja Stage. He sounded excited but I knew he was just happy to leave the office - sometimes sitting at your desk trying to bend a story into shape was such a drag.

I polished off my chicken and headed to the bus stop to meet Otieno, who was waiting impatiently for the adventure to begin. We boarded and took the back seat. Since it was not crowded, I gave Otieno the documents to peruse as we wound our way through ritzy Muthaiga on our way to Runda. Otieno read quietly, only occasionally pointing to an entry. I told him I would break it down for him as soon as we alighted.

The bus dropped us off. We took the side-walk and started towards Kamau's house. We talked about the documents and I gave him my theory on extortion. It was not a long walk but it took us through some really immaculate homesteads, the ones you see on travel magazines. Each gated entrance had a small stall adjacent to it that kept the guards protected from the elements. Others bore "*Mbwa Kali*" or "Beware of Dogs" signs strategically placed for any intruder or unwanted guest to see.

A guard wearing an ill-fitting khaki uniform met us at the gate to Kamau's residence. He wanted to know the nature of our visit. I flashed by badge and said it was important that I speak with his boss or the lady of the house as soon as possible. He took a long look at us as if trying to decide the best course of action.

"Just wait there," he said and disappeared into the little stall from where we heard him speak to someone on an intercom.

After a brief wait, we were ushered in through the gate and up the cobblestone driveway. The guard walked beside us holding his well-worn homemade nightstick in his right hand. I wanted to say something to him, anything but I could not find appropriate words.

A young maid, wearing a grey housekeeping uniform, complete with a tea apron, ushered us in through the mud room and into an airy sitting room where she asked us to sit and wait before she disappeared behind the foyer.

The sitting room was indeed quite cozy, soft white leather seats, a fireplace and family photos on the walls next to a well-stocked mini bar. I looked at Otieno who sat awkwardly on the love seat facing the hallway. I trained my eyes on the winding staircase that led upstairs to what I imagined would be bedrooms. This was what they called luxury, a far cry from my one bedroom digs in Dagoretti.

We did not wait for long before a man, who I assumed to be Kamau Kariuki, came sauntering down the stairs. He was well-built, almost athletic. He wore a light-brown leather coat, sleeves pulled up to his elbows, on top of a white tee-shirt and denim jeans, which looked rather odd for a middle-aged man. He walked almost deliberately slowly, holding onto the gold-plated railings on the winding stairwell. His receding hairline made his shiny forehead stick out like an eroded cliff. He had a ready smile that took over his bespectacled face. We stood up to shake hands.

"Good afternoon, gentlemen, to what pleasure do I owe this visit from two reporters?" he asked after our brief introductions.

He sat down beside me and leaned back on the couch. He flipped the leather jacket to the sides and I noticed he had a rotund mid-section. The maid came in and stood at the far end of the room, quietly, waiting for instructions.

"Cognac for me, Monica, and whatever these gentlemen may want," he offered.

Monica went over to the bar and poured a finger of cognac. I asked to have the same. Otieno said he would not mind a cold Tusker. Monica graciously brought our drinks and quietly slipped out of the room.

"Well, Mr. Kamau, we are here about Dr. Kizito," I started without mincing words.

With the mention of the doctor's name, he sat up quickly and the smile on his face disappeared momentarily. He took a sip of his cognac and tried to regain his composure.

"Yes, the doctor. I heard about him. What a tragedy. But why do you come to me?"

I was about to pull out the bank statement when the phone rang. Kamau excused himself. Otieno was sitting on the edge of his chair, holding his tusker between his legs. He had not taken a sip yet. I downed my cognac with one swoop and placed the glass on the coffee table. The drink warmed its way down my throat and all the way down into my stomach. It reminded me why I did not like liquor; because of the burning sensation it gives your insides. I shuddered and cleared my throat, trying to get the bitter after-taste out of my mouth. I felt for the bank statement in the inside pocket of my jacket. It was still there. Somehow, that felt reassuring. We sat there waiting for Kamau to return. The tension was growing by the minute.

He came back hurriedly. He pulled the specs from his face, wiped them with a handkerchief, and then put them back on, with his little finger sticking. He came up and stood right in front of us - akimbo. He smirked and said:

"Gentlemen, I'm afraid but I'm going to ask you to leave."

"But we have not discussed the reasons…"

He did not let me finish. He lifted his left hand towards his face and cocked his head backwards.

"I am not at liberty to discuss anything further with you. Monica, show these two out of the house and have the guard escort them to the gate at once!"

Before we could protest, Kamau walked out of the room. Monica came in and showed us out. We did not hesitate.

*   *   *

We made it back to the office and briefed Bulldog. He listened, quietly, with his index finger stroking his upper lip rhythmically. His face registered that puzzled look I had come to associate with either concern or irritation.

"I suggest you tail this Kamau Kariuki, find his associates, his businesses and everything else you can find out about him. I will get Jacob to drive you around beginning tomorrow."

He looked us over and without as much as another word picked up the phone and dialed a number. We walked out and went to the break room for tea and a review of the day.

Our visit had confirmed what we already knew - that Kamau had something to hide. But a more pertinent question was who had called him? No one would have known that we were with him unless someone had seen us go in - but who and why? I had been having that feeling that I was being followed and now I knew for sure - I had a tail. That, and the noose, did not make for a good feeling but it meant that we were on the right track.

Bulldog's offer of a company car and driver was most welcome. Perhaps Otieno said it best.

"No more public transportation, at least for a while. Plus, this Jacob is a really nice fellow, quiet, but nice."

I was just glad that I would not be alone when I was out there tracking this killer.

Jacob was the company driver. He ran all manner of errands for *The Daily Grind*. Whatever needed delivery from print paper, ink, office supplies to airport runs to pick up dignitaries. He was the go-to guy. Due to the nature of his work, he knew Nairobi and the surrounding metropolis well. He knew all the shortcuts to get from one side of the city to the other, and when to use particular highways to avoid traffic jams and construction delays. When all else failed, Jacob did not seem to mind breaking a few traffic codes to get to his destination.

"With Jacob, we have just added numbers to our side," I added. "I'll see you tomorrow, man. I'm off to meet Mburu."

CHAPTER THIRTEEN

The offer of company transport should have started today, I mused on my bus ride home. I sat next to a woman who, it turned out, had drank one too many, and she insisted on telling her invisible husband what he had failed to do for her in the bedroom.

I was not concerned about her loud complaints or her being drunk, hell; I could have used a few drinks myself. It was her bad breath, a mixture of stale breath and cheap alcohol, that got me. But fortunately, my mind wandered back to Kamau, the huge withdrawals and the mysterious phone call he had received that made him kick us out. Whoever he was, he was deep in this affair.

My stop came quickly, as things do when you are distracted. I jumped out as soon as the doors opened, squeezing myself between the other passengers who had also alighted. Amongst these was a man in a black sweater. I would not have paid him any particular attention except that after a few paces, I happened to turn my head to see if the bus had gone, only to find him staring at me but when our eyes met, he turned his back to me - quickly and deliberately. After about fifteen yards, I looked back to see if he had left. He was still standing there, with hands in his pockets, looking at me. He then turned away again. Could he be the person who had been following me all this time?

I decided to delay my walk home and let him be on his way first. So I fumbled for a cigarette, taking my time to light it. I looked closely at my watch and then felt about my pockets like I had lost something. He was not in a hurry either, straightening out his sweater and patting down his pants in what appeared to be delaying tactics. My heart began pounding. I felt warm all over. The image of the noose on my door came back. I pulled at my cigarette and let the smoke fill my lungs. Then I started walking away from the direction of my apartment - no need to box myself in. I glanced behind me. He was still following me. I added a little pace to my step without appearing to do so. After several hurried steps, I turned my head ever so slightly to look back. He was falling behind a little but still on my tail.

I crossed the road, heading towards Dagoretti Shopping Centre. I half-ran to avoid oncoming traffic but also to put some distance between me and the man in black. I was trying to get to Anne's Butchery off Karandini Road. It was a joint I frequented and where I knew I could then walk out at the back undetected and head back to the city. There was no way I was going to stay in my apartment tonight.

I walked into Anne's butchery. It was actually a beer den that also served roasted goat and beef made on order. It had four rectangular benches around wooden tables that served as the sitting area and in the front, a crudely built counter, complete with bar stools where revelers sat close to the source. A juke box in a corner blared out a soft benga-beat to which an older gentleman danced unsteadily by himself. I was about to head out to the back door when a voice startled me:

"Hey! What's up, man?"

I turned around quickly, and with relief, saw Mburu waving his arms frantically at me.

"Where are you going in such a hurry?" he asked as he stuck out his hand and pulled me towards him for a hug. "Or are you trying to skip on a bill? Come, sit down man and get yourself a beer."

He pulled me by the hand back to where he was sitting with two women, one of whom I recognised as Wanda. He had been courting her for some time. He introduced me to Helen, Wanda's friend. She was a pleasant looking woman and under different circumstances, I might have been more engaging but my eyes never left the door. I scrutinised everyone who walked in. I helped myself to some meat but I did not have the taste for it so I set it down on a napkin next to my beer.

Mburu noticed my preoccupation and commented, "What's with you, man? Is anything bothering you?"

I called him to the side and told him about my fight the other night, the noose and note, and now the man in black following me.

"Don't worry, cousin," he said, surprising me with his utter lack of curiosity for further details.

Instead, he felt inside his leather jacket, then patted it with his right hand and declared that we were in good company with 'Lucy.' I looked at him puzzled, and then at the girls who were talking animatedly about something. I thought he had introduced the other girl as Helen, not Lucy, and I said so.

"No, fool, not the ladies, my friend 'Lucy,' here," he said as he pulled my hand and placed it near his rib cage.

I felt a hard object. It was a gun. I withdrew my hand back quickly.

Mburu worked as an armoured truck driver with Wells Fargo Kenya Limited. His job entailed transporting loads of money from the Central Bank to all local banks in the city. They were an armed team of two: a driver and the money guy but I did not know that he carried a piece with him all the time.

"How long have you had that thing, man?" I asked.

He reminded me of the two times he had been ambushed after work, rumours having circulated that even when he was off duty, he carried loads of cash. Each time he had been beaten to within an inch of his life.

I had visited him at the hospital the second time. I remember I could not even recognise him from all the bandages on his face. His hands, broken in two places, were encased in plaster. He had suffered two fractured ribs and severe knife wounds. We never found out who did it but the scars on his face and body were daily reminders of the evil out there.

He told me that since he was not allowed to carry his regular weapon home from work, he had decided to get his own piece.

"I've never shot anyone and I hope I never do," he told me, shaking his head from side to side as if reliving the punishing beatings he had received. "But I promise you that anyone who lays a finger on me will have an early appointment with their maker!"

He then gave me a slap on my shoulder, thus closing the subject.

"Let's have a good time, eh? Don't you worry about a damn thing!" He flashed a huge smile and then winked - he was ready to party.

We walked back to the table, Mburu still amused by my reaction to 'Lucy.' I sat down and ordered another round for everyone. I was not in a hurry to go home, and my eyes were no longer trained on the door all the time. Helen must have wondered at my transformation from aloofness to vivacity. The rounds of drinks that just kept coming amidst laughter and the naughty jokes were quite a welcome distraction from my earlier ordeal. Mburu confident, armed and dangerous made me feel better about my situation. I invited them to my place and surrendered my one bedroom to Mburu and Wanda who went straight at it. Helen and I watched TV on a couch in the living room while trying to drown out the moans coming from behind the thin walls.

Eventually, despite the noises from the bedroom and Helen quietly snoring next to me, I managed to sleep. Actually, I had a much better sleep on the couch than I had had the previous night.

All would be well, I felt. We had 'Lucy.'

* * *

The morning came and with it a mild hangover. After we had all cleaned up, Mburu and I made breakfast: scrambled eggs, tea and buttered toast. We then made it to the bus station and into the city where we parted ways with Helen and Wanda. Mburu and I went straight to the office - no sign of the man in black following us.

I could tell Jacob was excited about his new assignment. He listened attentively as we briefed him. After I was done, I asked him if he had any questions.

"Yes," he said rather quickly. After a long pause he then asked: "When do we start?"

Otieno and I looked at each other and burst out laughing as we headed out to the parking lot to get the car. Mburu sat in the front with Jacob while Otieno and I took the back seat as we took off towards Kamau's house. It was exhilarating - I had never been on a stake out before.

When we got to Runda, Jacob drove about five hundred yards past Kamau Kariuki's gate, turned the car around and parked to the side, with two wheels on the sidewalk so that the car was tilted to one side. Jacob got out, opened the hood, took out his tool box and pretended to be working on the car. I had not thought about that and it made sense. You could not just park your car and chill out in Runda without raising eyebrows.

Otieno, Mburu and I lay low in the car but watched the gate for any movement, hoping that Kamau Kariuki would drive out. I was uncomfortable in my seat but the element of danger and the unknown made the discomfort tolerable. I felt like a detective. I wondered, is this what Ali did on occasion?

I was impatient for something to happen but Otieno was interested in hearing more about Mburu and Wanda. And he could not get over the fact that I had not made out with Helen.

"But you are like a camel, *bwana*," he said turning to me, holding back laughter. "I don't know how you do it."

I knew he was referring to my forced chaste life but I did not want to go there. It had been a dry season for me and the only woman I was really interested in was Meredith, but I had not yet summoned the courage to ask her out on a date.

"It's not by choice, *bwana* Otieno. Ask Mburu here. He can tell you about last night."

"But you did not even try. A woman is practically on your lap and you don't think to get some…" Mburu was clearly not helping me.

"Dude, we did not even click. Plus, I don't even know her. What if she is not safe? Do you know how prevalent HIV is amongst…?"

"Helen is Wanda's friend, not a hooker," Mburu protested. "You could have asked me for a condom. You know what that is, right?"

Both Otieno and Mburu were enjoying picking at me.

As we jostled, Jacob proved the more innovative. Tired of pretending to be doing things with the tool box, he got back into the car, drove and stopped by the gate, and got out of the car. He walked up to the guard post with some papers he had picked up from the car. Next thing we knew, he was talking with the guard on duty.

"Say, I have a delivery for a Mr. Kariuki. It is urgent that I get this to him pronto, something to do with courts and…"

"He is not here," said the guard. "He left early this morning for work."

Jacob feigned anger and disappointment. He paced up and down calling on the mercies of the almighty and cursing up a storm under his breath.

"I knew I should have come here early! I knew it!" he said, kicking at an imaginary enemy on the ground and yelling out Jesus' name.

"I really must get these to him. Tell me where I can find him. Or better yet, let me talk to his wife and ask her myself. She will understand the urgency. He is supposed to have these in his hands already!"

The guard, not to be blamed for delaying the receipt of the papers that needed to be in Mr. Kariuki's hands, gave Jacob an address where he could find him. Jacob thanked him profusely and promised that he would put in a good word for him with his employer for his help in this important matter. Then he hurriedly walked back to the car. The guard, smiling vaingloriously, waved at Jacob as he tore down the street towards the main entrance. We were headed towards the Kabete Technical Institute where, Jacob said, Kamau Kariuki had an office nearby; KayKay Concepts.

"How did you think of doing that?" Otieno asked after we had driven a short while. I was also impressed with Jacob's quick thinking. He did not answer. Instead, he shifted gears and all we could hear was the roar of the engine.

Jacob sped through Limuru Road back towards the city before taking a shortcut through the posh Muthaiga neighbourhood and onto Westlands. You could tell he was really enjoying himself by the manner in which he drove, perhaps believing that he was legally an undercover detective. I guess we all have our fantasies.

He then broke into a smile and said, "I figured we might be waiting there for a long while and still come out with naught," he answered, enjoying the roar of the car engine.

"What if he had said the boss was in?" I wondered.

"Then I would have given him the mail to deliver. It is addressed to Kalama Publishing House but came to us by mistake and I have had it in the car for about six months now. I've been meaning to send it back but have not gotten to it yet."

Just before Uthiru, we saw a huge billboard: KayKay Concepts. It had contact information. I took down the phone number and address to the main office. We made a right and drove in.

KenView was a relatively new neighbourhood, with luxury houses in different phases of construction, interspersed with completed units, each on a half-acre lot. They were built of cinder-blocks, complete with Spanish tiles. The front lawns were carpeted with Kikuyu grass and flower-gardens adorning the sides. As we drove down the main thoroughfare, we passed some empty lots in between fully occupied residences while others had *"For Sale"* signs boldly displayed on the gates. You could tell that the occupants here were just as loaded as the residents of Runda or Muthaiga.

We finally got to the model home which also acted as the office. There was a Mercedes Benz on the driveway in front of a nice green lawn with three young avocado trees stuck in the middle. The house was a two-storied ranch with hints of Spanish architecture accentuated by brownish-red brick roof tiles. It was a handsome house so to speak with no pretenses of opulence. Perhaps it was this simplicity that made it so inviting to the eye. We drove past the address, circled around and pulled over.

Jacob switched off the engine. There were so many missing pieces to this puzzle but we had the first piece. Would we find another to match the Kamau piece? I was not even sure how we had connected him to the serial killer except that Dr. Kizito had made a check out to Kamau Kariuki just before he was killed. Could it be a down-payment for a house built by KayKay Concepts? Was he blackmailing the doctor or even extorting money from him for something that needed to stay hidden? What if this was a coincidence? Well, no answer would come easily and perhaps these doubts were being occasioned by impatience. Good things come to those who wait, I told myself as I wiggled in my seat, digging in for a long wait.

I am not sure how long we sat there in silence. All I knew was that someone was having indigestion - the smell, when it came, was vicious. I suspected Jacob who sat stoically in the driver's seat, busying himself with the stick shift. I opened the window to let some fresh air in. Otieno gave me a look that told me he was suspecting me but I pointed to the back of Jacob's seat. He nodded his head and also rolled down his window.

Suddenly, a man walked out of the front door accompanied by a woman wearing what appeared to be a night gown. They were holding hands and laughing about something. Once they got to the Benz, they hugged, kissed and he got in the car. He backed out of the driveway and started towards the highway. The lady turned and hurriedly walked back into the house.

We followed the Mercedes Benz and before long we realised that we were headed back to Runda and to Kamau Kariuki's residence. It was our man. We drove slowly past his gate just as he pulled into his garage. The guard, who was now closing the gate, waved at us.

We had seen enough. We had a phone number for KayKay Concepts, number plates of his Mercedes Benz, and an address in

KenView where he was having a liaison with a female who undoubtedly was not his wife. These did not tell us how he had come to cash a check from Dr. Kizito, but they were more than enough to warrant further surveillance and scrutiny. We headed back to the office.

* * *

Bulldog was talking to a junior writer when we walked into the office. He stopped in mid-sentence and beckoned Otieno and I to follow him to his office. He sat down and listened, twiddling his thumbs impatiently, as we gave him a quick update.

"There has been another murder!" he blurted out before I could get to the details about the mystery woman. "It's your guy."

"What?" Otieno and I shouted.

He then gave us the details. The victim was a Mr. Ahmed Habib, an elderly man from the coast who owned an import-export clearing and forwarding agency. He had come to Nairobi to meet some contractors for bids on a building he was trying to renovate near Jomo Kenyatta International Airport.

I felt deflated, almost defeated. Here we were chasing a philanderer while the real killer was still at large. It was back to the drawing board - we were nowhere near bringing this whole thing to a close.

"Just when I thought we had him," Otieno said as we walked out of Bulldog's office.

I hated this feeling of having something yet having nothing. We were onto something, that was clear - but the path we were taking was long and winding. We needed something to give and lead us to the killer. The sooner he was apprehended, the sooner I would get my story and restore my life as I had known it - quiet, happy and dry.

CHAPTER FOURTEEN

● ● ● · ● ● ◉

Old habits die hard. I thought of calling Ali but decided against it. I knew that he would give me the same lines about professional boundaries. He was right on insisting that we should draw a line between his duty and mine, especially given the gravity of the situation. If he told me all he knew, I would feel obliged to also tell him all I knew and it was clear that we were not honouring our agreement to disclose - no hand was washing the other, each opting to hold onto some degree of autonomy.

Our professions were similar in this regard and as much as we could help each other, we could also hurt each other by compromising our sources. We could, of course, trade information where it served our different ends. It was a fickle balance that required judgment, a little daring, a little wit and a little luck. Besides, I had come to relish the idea of getting the story without his help - an audacious challenge but one I was coming to accept, perhaps misguided by a need to prove something to Ali.

The money trail had gone cold, at least for now. And with Habib's death I was pointed to another direction: the Coroner's office. There had to be something the Coroner had told the police which, for purposes of their own investigations, they were not releasing to the public - even an opinion. Ali had not given me anything from the Coroner's office. I knew he would be pissed off if he knew that I was going to talk to them. I had overstepped my boundaries with Wagateru and I was doing it again with the Coroner, but this was not the time for niceties.

Now it was time to dig under each and every crevice. I picked up my jacket. It was time to go visit the Coroner's office. I was going all out!

I caught the bus to the Medical Examiner's Office at the Hilton Bus Stop. Jacob was taking Otieno to see Mrs. Habib to dig for anything that might be of use. I just wanted to ask the Coroner a few questions and then get back in the office to join the team. We needed to piece it all together - it felt as though we had enough information to point us to the direction that would lead to getting the killer but we just needed a thread to tie it all together.

It did not take long to get to the Coroner's office. There was nothing that stood out to mark the building as a forensics center just outside the Kenyatta National Hospital. It would have been easy to miss it but for the occasional official crime scene police car or paramedic van driving in and out of the parking lot that surrounded the grey building.

I walked up to the front and entered through glass double doors. It was ominously quiet. Three leather seats, side tables and a magazine rack were all there was to the lobby – a dimly lit room of the two adjacent windows drawn up to reveal snowy opaque glass.

There was no one to usher me in so I wandered down the long corridor, lined with doors on either side that looked like domino pieces. The grey carpet was hard on the feet and looked well-worn, especially in the middle section where little threads of fiber stuck out haphazardly.

A little further down, I heard a sound, like a cabinet door closing.

"Hello," I called out, "Is there anyone here?"

No answer but as the door was ajar, I pushed it open and walked in. The strong scent of disinfectants brought memories of the products my mother used to bathe my wounds with when I was young. I hoped that I would not come across some dead guy lying on a table with their guts hanging out.

In front of me was a translucent curtain, with an opening in the middle. It swayed gently as if someone had just walked through it. I poked my head in. The room opened up to an unexpected vastness that took me by surprise. An operating table stood in the middle, an assortment of surgical equipment all around it. Cabinets, a desk complete with a computer, books and a reading lamp, lined the far end. And it was ice-cold.

I was about to turn around and walk away when I heard a toilet flush, some water running and then some paper rustling, accompanied by the unmistakable pitter patter of someone taking small steps on high heels.

"Hello!" I said a little bit louder, hoping to telegraph my presence to avoid any violent reaction. She came into full view, her hands in front of her as she patted them dry with a paper towel. She stopped briefly and stared at me, as if sizing me up before she continued walking towards me. She then threw the wet paper towel into a dust bin by the operating table.

"How may I help you?"

"Yes, my name is Jack Chidi. I am with *The Daily Grind*," I said, handing her my ID card instead of flashing it, but she waved it away.

"Oh, yes! I know who you are," she said. "You wrote about the City Murders." She sounded excited.

Well, I was getting quite a notoriety with the story. It felt good to be recognised but I did not want that to get to my head - I had always tried to keep a low profile but this was not bad either. I smiled, knowing that I had fans out there.

"I am looking for the Coroner. Perhaps you can point me to…"

"You are looking at her."

"You are the …?"

"What did you expect? A man, even an objective journalist such as yourself?" she asked mockingly.

She was obviously cherishing this. Since I did not have a defense for my unguarded bias, I muttered incoherently, hoping that she would put this matter to rest. But she looked at me, waiting. I had to say something, anything.

"Well, typically, most Coroners are …" I started but she interrupted me, much to my relief.

"Oh, please spare me the excuses. I understand," she said matter-of-factly, extending her hand in greeting.

"My name is Rosa. Rosa Alessandro."

"Nice to meet you Doc….."

"Call me Rosa."

"Rosa Alessandro…that name sounds familiar - Italian, right?"

She smiled at the way I let her name roll off my tongue.

"My father was Italian, so I am what you call a point-five. Do you know any Italians?" she asked but I could tell she was still mocking me.

"I knew of one - a Roberto Alessandro. You are not related to him by any chance, are you?" I asked, trying to lighten up the conversation and restore my image.

"You are good. I see you have done your homework," she said, smiling a little bit, all the while eyeing me.

"Really?" I was astounded. No way could it be her!

I first heard of Roberto during my days at the Senior Chief Koinange Secondary School. He was a floriculturist known for his extensive and innovative flower-breeding techniques. He had come to the country in the early nineteen seventies as a consultant for the flower industry. It was an industry that was already churning profits for farmers but with the introduction of chemical fertilisers, easier access to European markets and local organisation, the industry had ballooned into a multi-million dollar industry.

After three years, Roberto, who was now married to an Ethiopian-Kenyan, was alarmed to find that the flower industry was slowly morphing into a cartel of the wealthy, fattening their bank accounts only. Some just sat as board members, advisory committees or as directors of these conglomerates but raked in millions in kickbacks, sitting allowances and annual bonuses. Predictably, large scale farms began to swallow small enterprises by economic and physical force and subsequently drove local farmers into poverty.

Alessandro resigned from his post in protest and started a campaign to regulate the flower industry and make it environmentally responsible. He wrote and spoke extensively about the ways in which the flower industry was detrimental to sustainable development in and around the Lake Nakuru region. He even sent a report to the Minister of Agriculture that warned of the dangers of the overuse of chemicals in flower-farming. The chemical runoff from the flower farms had found its way into the rivers and underground aquifers and into the drinking water. Workers on these farms were also in great peril from organophosphate toxicity, low wages, unsanitary working conditions and even death.

The industry fought back with everything they had. They brought in their own experts, who countered every claim that Roberto had made with "facts". They began a sustained personal attack on Roberto and made sure that he did not find work anywhere in the country. By the time they were done with him, all he had left was a small house sitting on two acres where he lived with his wife and their daughter.

However, he did not give up. Instead, he started to lobby Environmentalist groups urging their respective countries to boycott flowers from the cartel. They took up his clarion call and begun demonstrations. The flower industry begun to hurt under such strong international scrutiny and even the government asked for more regulations as a way to parley the negative image of a Kenyan business.

The flower cartel and their wealthy business associates had had enough. Roberto had to be stopped. He died in a mysterious road accident one Sunday evening and his body was flown back to his home town in Sicily. The newspapers had carried a picture of his grieving wife and a wide-eyed daughter as they accompanied the casket back home.

Here she was now, the daughter, a full grown woman, a far cry from that mournful teenager in the papers.

I could tell that she was reading me, carefully, as if trying to make up her mind if I was to be trusted. People always did this with journalists - I had come to expect it so I allowed her time to make her assessment while I mentally caressed her youthful features. Not a bad trade off.

It was the symmetry of her eyes, the natural arch of her brows, complementing a chiseled jawline that captivated me. Her lips, nice and rounded, had just a hint of purplish-red lipstick, which made them appear moist and invitingly kissable. Her hair, long and braided into a long pony tail, dropped over her left shoulder, lazily, like a….

"Hey!" she startled me back to earth. "Come in and tell me what I can do for you."

She then took off her white coat to reveal a shapely figure.

She walked almost purposefully slowly, taking carefully measured steps. Her gait seemed familiar, like a model on a catwalk. She reminded me of the Miss Africa pageant in Mozambique that I had covered two years ago. Her body flowed elegantly as if in slow motion, her skirt gently hugging her rounded hips in perfect syncopation. It was like watching a living dream in colour. If she only knew what I was thinking! Perhaps Otieno was right; I needed to break my dry spell.

"So, tell me, what can do I for you, Mr. Chidi?"

"No, call me Jack or just Chidi," I chipped in.

She raised her eyes to me. I swallowed loudly. She smiled at my discomfort but I did not mind her toying with me, not at all. My eyes slowly strayed to her chest where two perky breasts stood as if in attention. Oh dear me - my mind was going to that happy place.

"Again, what can I do for you?" she asked, pointing at her face, telling me to focus my attention away from her chest.

"I am interested in doing a follow-up story about the murders. We still have not heard anything about the forensics. Is there anything you can tell me in regards to the manner of the deaths?"

I realised that I had not framed my line of questioning well. The problem was that I was trying to look and sound professional while also ogling her. Yes, she had me in knots but I still had a job to do.

"Have you found evidence of foul play or anything you would want to share with a hungry and frightened public? You know the rumours," I swallowed again.

"I'm not sure that I can discuss that with a newspaper man. Chidi, these are pending cases."

"I understand. Believe me, I do. I was just wondering how someone can die or be killed and there is no evidence of the cause of death?"

"Well, we know that they all died from a lack of oxygen or what we call generalised hypoxia. But we cannot conclusively say what caused the asphyxia."

She turned around and leaned over her desk, and her skirt rose to reveal her thighs. My eyes quickly darted to her legs - athletic but not muscular with faint dimples just above the knee joints. I steadied myself against the cabinet to my right and forced myself to look around the office. I did not want to be caught looking up her skirt. There was not much in here that held my attention long enough to stop me from stealing side-glances at her exposed thighs.

She pulled a folder from the top drawer and straightened up to face me. She flipped through some papers disinterestedly, licking her forefinger gently and delicately before turning a page. I inched closer to see what she was looking at but she closed the files quickly and placed them back in the drawer. I felt like I was being enveloped into an intoxicating world of seduction. It felt good to be here at this moment and I hoped it would last a while longer.

"So you know for a fact that they died from lack of oxygen. What could have ...?"

"Oh, Chidi, please do not ask me to speculate. The possibilities are endless, including erotic asphyxia. This office has not as yet been able to determine the agent or agents causing these adverse reactions."

She was now looking at me. I was not sure why but I felt my heart skip a beat. What if she liked me? After this mess was over, I would have to find a pretext to come back to see her again.

"By reactions you mean death?" I blurted out, trying to sound professional.

"Yes, genius, by reactions I mean deaths, at least in these cases."

She had caught me ogling again. I looked at my note pad and realised that I had not written anything. I pulled out my pen and scribbled some nonsense, all the while thinking of a follow-up.

"What is this office doing to get to a conclusive cause of death?"

"Well, we will continue running tests until we find out what caused the asphyxia. Right now, we have nothing," she said with a shrug of her shoulders. "Is there anything else I can do for you, Mr. Chidi?"

I liked the way she said it, almost flirtatious, and I allowed my mind to play around with the prospect of a date. Our eyes met and held for moment, forcing me to swallow a huge gulp of air. I quickly averted my gaze and walked clumsily towards the door.

My hands trembled as I reached for the door knob. I stopped, again trying to gather the courage to ask her to have a drink with me sometime. I had to ask her. I summoned all my powers but when I opened my mouth to do so, I froze.

"So what is the official statement regarding these deaths?" I uttered impulsively.

She smiled at the abruptness of my question, as if she guessed that it was not what I had in mind. I leaned against the door and pretended that I was holding a microphone to her mouth. She leaned over to talk to the imaginary microphone but not before she tilted her head, brushed the hair from her face with her right hand and tucked it behind her ear.

"We have concluded without a shadow of doubt from all the assays that they all died from generalised hypoxia, the cause of which is not known at this time."

Her smile completely warmed her face. I felt something in me stir and I knew it was time to leave.

I could not help but conjure up images of me and her enjoying some tropical drinks in Mombasa with the blue waters of the ocean lapping at our feet. Somewhere in my imagination, she turned into a genie and I started shrinking right before her smiling eyes. A loud horn and screeching brakes brought me back to reality as a car swerved in front of me. It missed me by inches. I had crossed the two lane highway without looking left or right!

I decided against going back to the office and so I headed towards home. A short bus ride later and I was in Dagoretti. It was a little early in the evening and I was not sure I wanted to spend all that time in my apartment. Not after that vision of Rosa and not with everything that I had gone through. Single life has its ups but being alone in an empty apartment is not one of them. A drink was not a bad idea so I headed to Anne's. In the morning, I was sure Otieno would brief me on Ahmed Habib's murder. I knew that the story would be the same as the other city murders. More than anything else, I needed to sit somewhere quietly and chart through all the pieces we had so far. There was so much to sift through, so much that had happened and despite my feelings of loneliness, I had work to do.

I was about to enter Anne's butchery when I saw a familiar figure, standing on the opposite side of the road facing me. The man in black was back!

I paused, thinking about my options. I decided to go in and then out the back door but something came over me - the 'animal' - and I found myself crossing the road towards him. I was going to confront him.

He had not expected this turn of events. He started backtracking. I hastened my step. He started half-running almost sideways, keeping an eye on me. I powered up to a sprint and he did the same. I gained some distance but he ran onto the street zigzagging through the traffic. Angry motorists rammed on their brakes, honking and cursing. I followed him across the street.

He jumped on to an unpaved path off the main street and I stayed in hot pursuit. He was at full sprint. My lungs were on fire but I needed to catch this motherfucker and for a few yards I was gaining on him. He looked behind and, realising that I was getting close, he cocked his head back and picked up the pace. Little puffs of dust rose behind him with each step. He looked like he was floating on air, his legs spinning faster and faster and carrying him away from reach. After a hundred yards, I gave up. I doubled over, gasping for air.

A little further ahead, he too stopped and held his knees with his hands in obvious anguish, facing me. We stood there, doubled-over, huffing and puffing. I tried to get a good look at his face but my eyes were blurry. I rubbed them and tried to re-focus. Nothing! I hoped to get a second wind and make a dash for him but the will to summon up any energy was gone. I was zapped.

After a few tense moments, he straightened up, gave me a little salute and began to walk away. All I could do was watch the man in black fade into the distance.

Somewhere, a dog was barking loudly. With my head hanging low on my neck, I staggered home, tired, angry, and despondent.

I had met the sublime and the ridiculous on the same day.

CHAPTER FIFTEEN

Several hours in the office the next day, Otieno ran to me holding a document which he placed in front of me, pointing his finger at it, as if it contained some dangerous chemical. He then walked around and stood over my right shoulder, still breathing excitely.

"Man, look at this! Look!"

The letterhead was from KayKay Concepts. I did not see what the big deal was as we already had this information.

"Read the damn thing, man!" Otieno said, irritated by my reaction or inaction.

It was some cover page of a brochure introducing the company, KayKay Concepts, to Real Estate agents in and around Nairobi. It highlighted several models of houses under construction, explicit with floor models, materials used for the interior décor and the exterior walls of the units. It also included a pricing guide for the different styles.

At the bottom of the letter was a list of board of directors in small print. I pulled the paper closer to my face. It listed Kamau Kariuki, Esther Wagio and Nahashon Juma as the Directors, followed by property listings. At the bottom of the page was a disclaimer about reproduction rights but I did not bother reading it. I looked up at Otieno.

"Where did you dig this up - from Mrs. Habib?"

"She would not speak to the press. I resorted to Google."

"You got this from the internet?"

"Yes, but the key thing is that KayKay Concepts is not a legally or officially registered company. I checked with the Registrar of Companies and Kenya Revenue Authority."

I thought about it for a moment. It did not really tell us all that much other than affirming that Kamau Kariuki owned KayKay

Concepts. It had also given us some new names: Esther Wagio and Nahashon Juma.

And then an idea hit me.

"What if there is a check from Habib made out to Kamau or KayKay Concepts? Then we can definitely say that there is a correlation between them and the murders. We can write our story and the police can take it from there."

"Oh, damn, man! I see where you are going with this," Otieno said. "But how do we do that without Mrs. Habib cooperating?"

I grabbed my jacket and headed out, with Jacob and Otieno right behind me. I knew just where to go.

I ran up the steps leading to the second floor of the Kenya Commercial Bank and into Agnes' office. Even before I could tell her why I was there, she had her hand held out.

"Hand it over."

"And a good morning to you too," I said as I handed her the printout.

She looked at it and let out a huge sigh. She then looked at me with those brown eyes of hers without a word. I liked this girl, her style. Too bad I stood no chance with her.

"I just want to know if there have been any more large deposits in Kamau Kariuki's accounts or in his company account if he has one," I whispered conspiratorially.

"Is there a deposit you are interested in in particular?" she asked while logging into the bank network.

I wrote down the names of all the murder victims, from King'ori down to Mr. Habib. My handwriting seems to have deteriorated with age, I thought as I tried to read what I had written. Either that or the adrenaline had usurped my penmanship. I asked Agnes for another piece of paper and carefully jotted down the names. I also jotted down the names of the directors, Esther Wagio and Nahashon Juma. I passed it on to her.

She kept punching numbers and writing figures on a note pad. She would then refer to the notes and then again key in a staccato of numbers and letters. She was working fast and I sat quietly. Deep down I was beginning to fear what we might find. It was one of those times - you hoped for the intended outcome and feared the consequences, all at the same time.

After a little while, Agnes printed out some pages, looked at them and handed them to me. I perused the documents carefully, scrolling my index finger along each entry. The veins on my forehead were throbbing and I could feel some perspiration forming on my brow. I jumped from my chair and gave Agnes a huge hug, thanking her for her help. She tried to wiggle herself from my tentacles but I was holding on tightly, lost in my aberration. After a little while, I became aware that I had held on to her longer than social decorum allowed. I let go, smiling sheepishly as if in apology. She just waved me off. I ran down the steps and into the waiting car.

"We have the proof!" I told Otieno, handing over the bank statements.

He read them, making disapproving sounds with his mouth after each entry. After a while he sat back on the seat looking straight ahead in almost resigned exasperation.

"Son of a bitch!" he burst out. "It's him!" He was not grinning. "What next?"

"I think we should confront him."

"Shouldn't we get Ali in on this, Jack?" Otieno asked somberly.

As I gave it some thought, I called Mburu and asked him to meet us. Otieno had a point but if we called Ali, we would have to wait for an official briefing. It was not like he was going to take us with him to arrest Kamau. Plus, we still did not have fool-proof evidence. All we had were illegally obtained bank statements.

We picked up Mburu at the Polytechnic briefed him. Far from being disappointed that we were not going for drinks, he became elated, a thin smile caressing his lips. He felt for his inside jacket as if to make sure we were in good company. Then he nodded, and with that, we headed out towards Runda.

At the gate, the watchman, still wearing the same uniform from the other day, stood his ground, aggressively alert to his gate-keeping duties.

"You are making another delivery?" he asked Jacob sarcastically after we had pulled up.

"Not today. But we are here to see Mr. Kariuki. Please let him know the journalists are back," I chimed in.

The guard looked at us briefly and went to the intercom. After a few minutes, he returned and opened the gates and we drove in. None of us had expected that we would be allowed to go in so readily, especially after our last encounter. I started feeling apprehensive again and this time Mburu and 'Lucy' did not assuage my fears. I guessed it was only natural. Only fools walk into a death trap with smiles on their faces.

Kamau was waiting for us by the door and ushered us into the sitting room. We sat down and he asked the maid to get us some drinks. I declined, opting to keep a clear head. He sipped his cognac.

"You have been quite busy," he stated.

I was not sure why he expected anything else or why he felt the need to let us know this. Or, I thought, perhaps he was letting us know that he was privy to what we had been up to. Whatever the case, I knew I needed to remain calm - or the appearance of nerves of steel.

"Yes, we have. How about you, have you been keeping well?"

"I'm a busy man when I need to. As you can see, I keep my own hours," he said twirling his glass for emphasis. "But enough chitchat. I did not expect that you would return, so when I heard you were here, I figured you must have pressing matters to discuss."

He put his glass down, crossed his legs and adjusted his pants, hiding his ashy ankles. Then he looked directly at me. He was smiling

- but his eyes could not hide an irritation that bordered on anger. I assumed that his patience would last long enough for him to find out what we had on him.

I pulled out the paper Otieno had given me with the property listings. I looked at it and paused. He squirmed in his chair, not knowing what I was holding in my hand. I then passed it on to him. He stared at it, then, recognising what it was, his face softened. He uncrossed his legs and reached for his cognac, relieved.

"You came all the way to hand me this? Surely, you are not interested in housing, are you?"

"I would like to purchase one someday but I want to stay alive long enough to see it," I said.

He sat up sharply. The smile disappeared from his face momentarily. Realising that he had betrayed his cool, he tried to play it off by sipping on his cognac and shuffling his feet before crossing them again.

"A house is a good investment. It takes away a lot of stress," he said, trying hard to stay calm.

"I guess it does. I guess it does. The check Dr. Kizito wrote to you: was he buying a house from you?" I asked almost spontaneously.

He busied himself again with his cognac, racking his brain for an answer that would sound rational, casual without arousing suspicion or inviting follow up questions.

"I do not know all the details of our operation. You can check with our accounts department."

"Just tell us about the check the good doctor made out to you!"

"I am not at liberty to discuss company matters with you. Or anyone else for that matter."

His voice was a little shaky. We were getting somewhere.

"But your company is not registered," interjected Otieno, who had been quiet until now.

"My company is registered. I have no idea what you are implying," Kamau retorted, looking long and hard at Otieno as if trying to intimidate him but Otieno stared right back at him.

"We checked everywhere, including the Ministry of Trade and Commerce, the Revenue Authority, Business Registry - no one has ever heard of KayKay Concepts."

The room was deathly quiet as we waited for an answer. I was hoping that he would involuntarily say something that would confirm what we had. Although we had the bank statements proving motive, we still did not have anything concrete to tie him to the murders. We needed his willing or unwitting cooperation.

"What is this to you anyway?" he asked after a while.

"We are investigating murders!" It was Otieno again.

"Oh, I see. I had no idea that journalists were in the police business," he said with a sneer and stood up quickly.

Mburu, with an agility that belied his general demeanor, shot up and placed his hand inside his jacket, casually indicating that he was armed.

The cold menacing look in his eye was not lost on Kamau who sank back into his seat and reached for his cognac. He looked puzzled, defeated and unsettled but he was careful not to say anything self-incriminating. He finished his cognac and poured himself another stiff one. It was a chess game, we thought we held the advantage, but so far, and despite the fear, he was not breaking.

"Mr. Kamau, you're up to your neck in this mess. Mr. King'ori writes you a check, he is murdered, and you cash it the next day. Dr. Kizito writes you a check on the night he is murdered, you cash it the following day. The same thing for Professor Obo and Solstice Wakaba - check, murder, and cash. What I don't understand is why you had to kill them."

"I did not kill anyone!" Kamau thundered, "I will not have…."

I decided to push it.

"Soon we will find out that you gave Mr. Habib the same treatment - check, murder…"

He shot up wagging his finger at me.

"You all need to get the fuck out of my house. Get out! Get out! You come in here, insult me and accuse me of murder?"

Spittle was shooting out of his mouth with each word. He started towards me, the veins on his forehead now prominently carved out in anger. Before he could take a second step Mburu stood up and pulled 'Lucy' out. This is not what I had in mind but we had taken it as far as we could.

"We are taking all these documents to the police," I said to him after a moment's silence.

He slowly sunk to his seat, still staring at 'Lucy,' and I could tell he was contemplating his next move.

"Go ahead. If you had anything tangible, you would have gone to the police already."

"Well, we are just about to but first, we are running a special edition of *The Daily Grind* with your picture front page and center."

I slapped the papers with my left hand for emphasis. I saw his face cringe, his eyes open wider. Something had struck a nerve.

"Hey, wait a minute!" he pleaded, genuine terror in his voice and eyes, looking up at Mburu submissively.

Mburu lowered the gun and took a step back.

Kamau, now breathing a little heavily, choked on his own saliva and started coughing uncontrollably.

"I am not a murderer," he said after his coughing fit, "I do not have anything to do with anything. Whatever you write will be false and I will sue you for libel."

He looked lost, almost pitiful, but his voice sounded almost sincere.

"Listen, if you did not kill them, then who did it?" I asked. "You are an accomplice to murder either way."

"I swear I did not kill anyone. You can kill me if you want but I am innocent."

He walked over to the bar and instead of pouring himself another drink, he pressed on the intercom button. I knew at once that he had summoned the security guard. The last thing we needed was being cornered in his house. And we had gotten what we wanted: we had our man. Otieno and I could break the story, and Ali could take over from there. We walked out, jumped in the car and headed back to the city. We had a story to write.

* * *

We literally ran to Bulldog's office with the scoop. This time, he did not even let me start. His eyes told me we were in for another shocker.

"It's happened again. There has been another murder, different, but murder all the same."

This was getting ridiculous. I felt my knees buckle. I pulled a chair and sat down.

"What the hell? Who is it now?"

"Wagateru!"

CHAPTER SIXTEEN

● ● ● · ● ● ●

Wagateru had been shot once in the head at point blank range - an execution. His body was found at the western entrance of Uhuru Park but it was not clear whether he had been shot there or the killer had just dumped his body there. Why would anyone want the hawker dead? Perhaps it was to silence him. But, surely, if he had any information pertinent to the investigation, I'm sure Ali would have put him in protective custody. It was standard protocol and Ali was a stickler for following procedure. So why was he dead?

It had to be a mistake; the only thing enjoining Wagateru to the City Murders was the surveillance tape which, Ali had ascertained, had nothing to offer the investigation. But here he was, dead after he had been picked up by the police, released and then presumably picked up again by unknown people, assuming that the mango seller was right in what she saw. His execution did not fit the pattern of wealth, hotels, social power, and checks, which ruled out Kamau as his killer. Or did it?

I had expected that Kamau would do something in reaction to our visit and rough encounter in retaliation. This was really just a long stretch trying to tie him to Wagateru's murder.

I was in the office mulling over all the possibilities when my phone rang. It startled me but I picked it up before it rang a second time.

"Hello."

There was no answer so I said hello again. There was still no answer and I was about to hang up when a muffled voice came on.

"You've been a very busy boy, Jack. I hope you liked the tie I left for you!"

"Hey, who is this?" I whispered loudly.

"We've been watching you and we won't let you get away this time!"

"What do you want?" I was really freaking out.

"You will find out soon enough. And by the way, how is Meredith? Have you seen her lately?"

Click! The phone went dead.

I sat there for a minute with the phone still in my hand. My heart began racing and a fear washed over me. I replaced the phone on its cradle and sat back on my chair. Okay, this had taken a turn I had not expected. My attack from the other night, the noose on my door, the man in black, Wagateru dumped near the pond and now Meredith! How did they know about Meredith and how I felt about her?

I reached for my phone to call her, to make sure she was okay but I realised that I did not have her number. Damn, man! Okay, I would call New London and ask to speak with her. I logged on and searched for New London Grill. It is in moments like this that you wish for high-speed internet connection.

The investigation had taken a personal turn but it also confirmed that I had touched a very raw nerve at the center of the city murders and they wanted me to stop. Why should I stop doing my job? It would be like a criminal asking a police officer, on threats of harm, to stop investigating their crimes. I had come this far, I felt close to the quarry, and I was on the right side of the moral equation. It was time to call my buddy, Ali Fana - I had taken this as far as I could.

I had not talked to him recently, respecting that professional boundary he had laid out, but I would be a fool not to ask him for help now. My life and the lives of those around me were in danger. It was also time for updates before we broke the story of KayKay Concepts and their connections to the murder victims. I too had some information to give him. We were both after the same thing after all but our egos had seen to it that we keep each other at arm's length for the most part.

Although I felt strongly that I had every right to question whoever and however, I was also cognizant of the fact that I could blow this case by not involving law enforcement, thus letting the killer or killers go scot free. We had Kamau Kariuki and his company cornered, but we could not make any more moves with what we had. I would ask Ali to fill me in and he, using his professional judgment, would decide what he could disclose without jeopardising his investigation of the murders.

I called him and he agreed to meet me outside Tratorria Restaurant on Kaunda Street.

Just then, the New London Grill website popped up on the screen and I wrote down their phone number. On my way to meet with Ali, I dialed the number but I got a busy signal. I would try again later. I had to get in touch with Meredith.

I was walking to my meeting with Ali when I caught myself looking behind my shoulders to see if I was being followed. It was then that I realised how much this story was affecting my lifestyle. A few days ago, my life had been ordinary, with no fears of harm except the usual awareness of surroundings, pickpockets, avoiding dark alleys and drinking joints far from the central business district. It revolved around going to work, trying to find a way to court Meredith and the occasional family reunions. It was a mundane existence but one that had served me well. Life in the big city for me meant knowing your favourite haunts and sticking to your familiar territories without deviating.

Here I was now, scared for my life and numerous questions swirling like mini-tornadoes in my mind. Who had just called? Were they just checking to make sure I was at the office so they would ambush me on my way out? Why was Wagateru killed? Could it have been because of me? Was it perhaps to send me a message? Okay, this was a stretch - it was not as if he and I were acquainted with one another.

We sat in a corner booth and I told Ali about the phone calls. He listened patiently. After I was done, he looked almost sad. I knew that even he had not anticipated that they would come after me like this.

"Man, it's because of scenarios like this that I've been telling you to slow it down a tad and let the police handle this. These guys can be ruthless."

From the tone of his voice I knew that he was sincere.

"Well, what do I do now? They are after Meredith, man!"

I said fumbling for a cigarette, my hands shaking a little. Ali pointed to the "no-smoking sign" by the counter.

His face softened and then, looking at me with pleading and concerned eyes he said, "The only one thing I can tell you Jack is chill, you know, take it easy for a while. It won't be long before we break this thing wide open and like I promised, the story is all yours."

"Have you found anything on Wagateru, or the others?" I asked, seizing the opening.

"You are quite something. But I know the feeling." He chuckled and then continued, "I am not handling his case but I can see a possible connection." He looked at me again and then smiled. "Are you sure you don't want to take it easy for a little while? You look like shit!"

"I am an investigative journalist. I ask questions..."

"Yes, I know you want the story, but this is getting out of hand, but don't quote me on that."

He then leaned forward towards me, and whispered, "Do you have anything for me?"

So I told him we were looking into KayKay Concepts and that we had found a possible connection - the huge sums paid out by the victims just before they died. I told him that we were going to print with the story as our lead.

"No, no, no please don't! We are onto them. Just don't print anything just as yet. We think we might be able to spring some arrests."

"So you also think Kamau is our guy?"

"I can't say for sure but just sit tight. We know all about this fellow. We know about the checks. We are very close to making a link that can hold up in a court of law. That's why we have been quiet."

"I'll have to talk with Bulldog but I'm sure we can sit on it a little longer."

"I am so glad you mentioned this because we can't afford to have this case blow up in our faces. How did you know about Kamau Kariuki anyway?"

I gave him a little chuckle.

"I can't tell you my sources."

"You are one arrogant son of a bitch, you know that? You were about to blow one of the biggest murder cases....."

"What are you talking about?" I interrupted.

"You never think of anyone else but yourself. You think you know it all because you are a big shot journalist!" He was whispering, but it was loud.

"What the hell are you talking about? Are you jealous of me, man?" I asked incredulously.

"You see that's just it - you think you can always do whatever you want, however you want to and with whomever. You have never once stopped to think of how your actions affect others."

"Dude, is this about Zuleika?"

"What do you think? That was my kid sister you were messing around with!"

"Ali, that was years ago, man."

"It does not change the fact that you were... you were...." he could not bring himself to say it and I did not want to finish it for him.

"It's not like she was a child," I said thinking to myself that I should tell him that she was no Mother Theresa.

Suddenly, I felt the urge to hurt him, to destroy this image he had of his sister once and for all. But I restrained myself, saving it for another time. Could it be that I was the one being driven by jealousy and resentment? Zuleika had left me and I'm sure that Ali played a big role in that break up.

"That was a long time ago," I said trying to cool down. "You couldn't possibly be carrying this burden all these years, man, could you? Let it go. Jeez, man!"

He looked hurt but I was not sure that I needed to apologise. I had said my piece and that was all I was going to say about the Zuleika affair. Just now I needed him, or rather his job, more than he needed me or mine.

Then I came up with the first gesture of reconciliation.

"How are Fatima and the kids?" I asked after we had cooled off a little bit. I sometimes felt as if we could make a great partnership if we learned to accept that we were both professionals and not competitors.

Ali too had regained his composure. He explained that working late nights was taking a lot of his time away from his family and he missed being able to have dinner with them. He looked tired and I could only imagine what it must be like to have an anxious city looking up to you to capture an elusive serial killer.

We chitchatted cordially for a few more minutes before he stood up to go. He apologised that he could not provide me or Meredith with a security detail. The best thing would be for me to lay low until they had apprehended the culprits. He promised to call me when he had more information and hopefully an arrest.

"You still get the exclusive," he said.

"That will be great, man, I truly appreciate it." I was sincere.

As soon as I went back to the office, I called Meredith, and again the number was busy. I asked Otieno and Jacob to accompany me to the London Grill but she was nowhere to be found. I talked to one of the workers who assured me that she was expected that evening.

I handed her my card and urged her to have Meredith call me emphasising that it was really important. We got back in the car. I called Mburu and told him about the threats.

"Don't worry, JC, I have your back. Just tell me when you need me."

"Let's meet up and see this thing through. It's time to pull all the stops."

I had a talk with Jacob and Otieno. If anybody needed out, this was the time - no questions asked and no hard feelings. No one would hear of it despite the threats. We shook hands - the posse was ready. It was time to ride. And we had to ride hard and fast!

CHAPTER SEVENTEEN

The mood in the car was somber. It was like we all knew that we were playing the back nine. First, we were going to visit Kamau's mystery lady at KenView - the model house. We were going to rattle each cage until we found what we were looking for.

If this was the work of a gang, who was behind them? What was their motivation? Was it possible that the crime scenes were being staged, that the victims were murdered elsewhere and then brought into motels?

I had more questions than answers. Kamau Kariuki was the link, the bridge to solving the crime and we needed to get to him by closing in on all his dealings. He was the weak link that would crack under pressure.

We had not gone far into our drive up Uhuru Highway towards KenView when I saw Jacob taking long glances on his rear-view mirror. I looked behind me but I did not see anything sinister. I guess he was just being precautious, which made me feel better knowing that everyone was on high alert - the game had changed for good and we needed all eyes, all the time.

Just after we had gone past Westlands Shopping Centre, Jacob announced that we had a tail, a black Range Rover, four cars behind us. He stepped on the accelerator and we surged forward, weaving between two cars in front of us. The Range Rover was hot on our heels, easily covering the distance between us but opting to stay about three hundred feet behind.

In an effort to shake them off, Jacob made a quick right turn onto Waiyaki Way and jumped in front of two tractor trailers. After this, he went speeding down the hilly road, winding down past Msongari Convent and then wound his way back onto Waiyaki Way. Jacob, looking quite pleased with his evasive tactics, smiled as we sped away. I looked behind us and saw that he had lost them.

A few minutes later, the Range Rover was on us again at a conspicuous distance. They clearly were not trying to stay concealed. Mburu reached out and pulled 'Lucy' from his shoulder holster, dropped the clip to check for bullets and locked it right back, pulled the hammer and held her between his legs.

"Jacob, I need you to follow my instructions to the letter. When I give you the signal, I want you to stop the car quickly right in the middle of the highway. And I want everyone to stay down."

I looked at Mburu. He had a look I had not seen before, a cross between determination and resignation. We were in some deep shit. We had one gun between us against a gang that was probably well armed. I felt a tightening in my chest and my breathing got heavier. Otieno kept looking back at the Range Rover but he still had that damn grin on his face!

"Ok, now!" Mburu shouted as we rounded off a corner just past Nairobi School. Jacob jammed on the brakes and we were lunged from our seats sharply. The car skidded to a halt amidst the screeching and honking from the other drivers, some of whom were forced to drive over the curb into the bushes.

Not expecting this, the driver of the Range Rover was slow to react. He rammed on his brakes forcing a loud screech followed by smoke as the four tires burned against tarmac. The vehicle came to a full stop within one hundred feet of us. Mburu jumped out, cocked his gun and pointed it at the Range Rover.

"Keep your hands where I can see them!" Mburu shouted, barking orders at the driver of the Rover. He was walking towards it cautiously, the gun never wavering from the driver. I turned around in my seat and looked out through the rear window. The driver had his hands on the steering wheel, the engine still running. He revved the car loudly but he looked indecisive, and I thought he might try to run Mburu down. I peered to the passenger's side and that's when I saw him, the man in black! Without giving it much thought, I jumped out and rushed towards them - the 'animal' was aroused!

Mburu was approaching the driver's side when the man in black opened fire. I ducked and ran back to our car. Mburu let out two shots in quick succession before taking cover. We received fire from the Range Rover and I heard the shattering of broken glass and then felt the shards of glass flying all around us. Other drivers gunned their cars and drove over the embankment and onto opposite traffic heading back to the city. Clanks of metal against metal, screeching tires, screaming men and women running for cover behind nearby bushes, ceaseless honking, shouting and gunfire – total mayhem!

The driver of the Rover backed up and crashed into two cars behind him. He then shifted forward and gunned his sports utility vehicle past us, narrowly missing Mburu who got down on one knee as they passed us, his hands outstretched in front of him and let out six or seven shots in such quick succession that they sounded like one reverberating clap of thunder. The bullets shattered the back window of the speeding vehicle as it raced into the distance.

We jumped back into our car and gave chase. Jacob's eyes were transfixed on the road, his body rocking back and forth as if trying to add a little bit more horse power to our car but after three miles at high speed, we lost the sports utility monster. Mburu was pensive. He reloaded 'Lucy' and put her back into his holster.

"Do you all know what this means?" Mburu asked.

There was silence. We looked at him the way school children look at their teacher who has just announced that the test results are out.

"It means that they are now playing for keeps," Mburu answered himself. "Next time they will shoot on sight. No more scare tactics. The game has changed for good!"

That jolted me back to the reality that we had just been shot at. Some people had just tried to kill us! The man in a black sweater, who had followed me the previous evening in Dagoretti, had opened fire on us. It did not matter that Mburu had drawn his gun first.

"Should we report this incident to the authorities at Kabete?" Otieno asked as we turned around at Uthiru Shopping Center.

"No, I don't think that's a good idea – there'll be too much explaining," Mburu answered.

We were now near KenView Estates. There was no turning back now. We had to proceed with our original plan. We pulled up to the model house. Kamau's car was not there. It was not him we were after but the lady we had seen him with. Jacob stayed in the car with the engine running while Otieno and I walked to the front door. Mburu stood by the main entrance, watching out for any unwanted visitors, his right hand cradling, 'Lucy'. We were no longer taking chances. We had to be vigilant. The stakes in this case had just been raised significantly.

I knocked at the door and waited. I heard shuffling noises inside and then the sound of the front door unlocking. It was the housekeeper, going by her *merry maids* uniform. She looked at us but did not say a word. I extended my hand and asked her who would be showing us the house. She looked puzzled. To sound like I knew what I was talking about, I told her we had just made a last minute appointment and were told to come and just walk in.

"I spoke with the lady who was here yesterday and she said it would be okay," I went on.

"Oh, it's okay," said the housekeeper, relieved. "She will be here to show you the house. She is never late for her appointments."

We excused ourselves and walked out, saying we would drive around and get a feel of the neighbourhood. We headed back in the car to regroup. We would wait at a distance, hidden from sight until the realtor showed up.

We were now getting to meet the players in this game of death. I still felt vulnerable - they had an advantage - they knew who we were and where we lived and they were trying to eliminate us. We were getting close - too close for comfort. On the other hand, we were at the cusp and there was no turning back: it was either us or them - and somebody was going down for the count.

We did not wait for long. A blue BMW drove to the model home and pulled up at the short driveway. A woman stepped out of the luxury car and walked into the house. We all recognised her as the woman we had seen with Kamau. She had that stride of confidence and sensuality that invited you to think of actions that did not invoke one's piety.

We were about to drive up when another car came speeding down and pulled in. It was Kamau's Mercedes Benz. He walked up to the front door and let himself in. After a little while, the door opened and the housekeeper walked out with her bag and headed towards the main entrance. I guessed she was done for the day or was simply on her way to the market or something as convenient as that.

We sat silently, each lost in deep thought and imagination about what was happening inside the house. My mind went briefly to visit with Meredith. I hoped she was alright. After all this was over, I was finally going to ask her out on a date. It would be nice to kiss her, I mused. She awakened something in me that Linda had almost destroyed.

I remembered Rosa. She was beautiful and seductive but seemed a far cry from my world. Would she really go out with me for real, I wondered? I felt like I was betraying Meredith but I reminded myself that there was really nothing between us, as of yet. Was this what Ali was referring to as selfishness? Nah, it could not be. Ali was just hypersensitive. I thought about telling Otieno about my conversation with him but that was going to have to wait.

After about half an hour, Kamau walked out holding hands with the mystery lady. She no longer had the beige suit but a *kanga* wrapped around her shoulders.

Otieno smacked his lips loudly and said, "That, my friends, is some real estate!"

He was staring wide-eyed again. I had never gotten used to Otieno's penchant for voyeurism.

Kamau and the lady talked for a little while and then kissed briefly before he got in the car and drove off. She hurriedly walked back into the house.

"A classic hit and run," Otieno observed, his wide grin cutting across his face.

We waited for several minutes and then drove up to the gate. Otieno and I got out, walked to the front door and knocked. There was no answer but we waited patiently. I could hear what sounded like water running, like someone was taking a shower. We waited until the sound quietened. Then we knocked on the door again, a little louder. This time the door opened and the woman, now back in her beige suit, stood right there in front of us. I could not believe my eyes.

It was Fatima, Ali's wife! How had we failed to recognise her?

Coming face to face with us now, her face dropped. She started to slam the door shut but I stuck my foot out and trapped it. I pushed myself in and Otieno followed. She walked backwards with her hands outstretched to her sides, trying to hold onto something. Her eyes registered fear and shock. Otieno stared at her, shaking both hands in the air, his mouth aghast but no sound came. He turned around and slammed his open hands against the wall with a loud bang.

"What is this? What do you think you are doing?" he asked, his voice quivering. He turned to face Fatima who now had her back on the kitchen counter facing us. She did not answer. Her chest heaved back and forth in short bursts.

"What the hell is going on?" I asked. "Oh, my god, what have you done, Fatima? What have you done?" My heart was pounding; I was lost, angry and trying not to believe what we had just witnessed. Ali - why would she do this to him?

"I...we...I sell real estate and I am waiting....you know, for buyers so I can show..."

"Does Ali know what you are doing? Does he know you are ...?" I could not bring myself to say the words. But how could he? I felt bad for him.

She raised her finger and pointed at me.

"I think you better leave!" she yelled. "This is none of your business!"

She looked ashen, cold and confused. She was in a tight corner and like a cornered animal she was beginning to fight back.

"Jesus Christ, Fatima, what were you thinking? Is this how you sell real estate?" I asked sarcastically.

"You don't know anything!" she started. "That man was just here to drop some information and…"

"Spare the bullshit for your husband!" I now shouted. "That man, that man is Kamau Kariuki. Do you even have an idea what he has done; do you even fucking know who he is?"

My mind was racing, trying to make sense of all this crazy turn of events. How was I going to tell Ali that his wife was screwing some bastard who might be involved in the very murders he was investigating? I thought about calling but how was I going to break news of this magnitude…where does one even begin?

"If you don't leave right now, I am going to call the police!" she threatened.

"Shut up! Shut up!" I noticed I was shaking.

"No, just let her call the police. Perhaps Ali will respond and we can tell him everything," Otieno replied, his grin gone.

"Do you know that Kamau…do you know that your husband is investigating him for murder?" Otieno went on.

"Murder?" she asked looking at Otieno. "What murder?"

Otieno was beside himself. I had never seen him like this. He was fuming, pacing up and down. I knew he was thinking the same thing I was: how would we break this to Ali? Should we even tell him? Of course we had to tell the man - what kind of friends would we be if we did not?

I knew that once Ali found out, he was going to kill the bastard - I knew his temperament - Kamau was a dead man walking! But what was he going to do to the mother of his children? That was something I did not want to know!

Fatima suddenly turned around, grabbed her handbag and car keys and ran out. I followed, hoping to stop her but she pulled out before I could get to her. She backed out of the driveway and sped towards the highway. I dashed back into the house. Perhaps there was something here that would help us tie everything together.

Otieno was already rummaging through loose papers and files he had found on the dining room table. Most of them were pamphlets, showcasing the different luxury homes. There was a sheet with pricing, some blue prints, delivery invoices and material orders. To the left of the table was a tall cabinet with six drawers filled with files. They were arranged alphabetically, back to front with neatly labeled tabs. I did not know which files I wanted to look at so I just browsed through the labels, pulling this one and that one randomly.

"Hey, look here," Otieno said after we had dug around for a little while.

I walked over to where he was. In his hands he held a rolodex with all kinds of names and addresses and including phone numbers. Amongst the many names in the rolodex were those of Isaac King'ori, Dr. Kizito, and all the other victims. It was information we already had. We needed more, something to link KayKay Concepts and all its directors to the city murders. What was this missing link? Whatever that was, we were certain that it would be found here.

I went back to digging through the file cabinet. I came across a folder marked "Articles of Incorporation." I opened it up and perused through it. They looked official. Nothing sinister about this but it was a blank application. I put the folder back and pulled another one labeled 'finances.' There were entries in this document that did not make sense. On the back of the folder there was an envelope. It was addressed to Kamau and Sons Contractors from the Superior Administrative Courts in Mombasa. It was a bankruptcy notice.

An injunction had been issued against this company doing business as Kamau and Sons Contractors, an entity based in Mombasa. They had been ordered to pay their creditors millions of shillings and all assets associated with Kamau and Sons Contractors had been seized and placed under receivership. Strapped for cash, the son of a bitch had simply relocated to Nairobi, started an unregistered company and was conducting an illegal business in the capital city with all impunity! But how did that translate to the killings or murders?

We had already spent enough time here so I beckoned Otieno for us to leave. We ran out, jumped in the car and sped away.

We had had quite a day so we decided to deviate from our usual drinking haunts and go to a dive somewhere else in town. We all needed a drink and we needed to stay alive.

I was still reeling from finding out the infidelity of Ali's wife. How could he not know? But then again how could he? I felt sorry for him. He doted on his family and was always talking about them. I too felt betrayed when I remembered the days we all got together either in town or at their home.

"That is why I'll never get married," Mburu confided, revealing that we all had the same thing in mind. "There is too much bullshit going on and the stakes are too high."

Mburu looked at us in anticipation, as if waiting for affirmation. None came so he shrugged his shoulders and lit a cigarette.

"What about Wanda?" I asked.

He looked at me for a while as if wondering why I was really asking that question. Then he grinned widely and returned to sipping his beer. Everyone was trying to make light of a very desperate situation.

"Oh, I see you have not forgotten about my Wanda. I hope we did not keep you awake but that's how you put it down!" he said breaking into loud laughter. He turned to look at me. "How come you did not get with Helen?" he asked amidst laughter.

I did not respond as my mind had strayed to the vision of the Coroner and then back to Ali's wife. What in the world would Ali do when he found out? She had let me down badly too; she was always what I would have wanted in a wife, and now this? How long had she been having this affair?

"Have you two met up again?" It was Otieno, seeking more details from Mburu about Wanda.

"Why are you so preoccupied with other people's sex life?" Jacob asked. "Are you having difficulties in that department? You should try that Viagra thing, man; I hear that shit keeps you up for four hours straight, like this." He extended his right arm across the table for illustration. That, coming from Jacob was hilarious! The man had no sense of humour in him.

We bantered over drinks for about two hours and ordered some roast goat and *ugali* for a late lunch. After the rather fatty meal, we headed out. We were very conscious that we were not out of danger. The crucial thing now was to lay low and hope for something to come up that would tie things together. We had done as much as we could with what we had. It felt as though we had come to a brick wall and the answers we sought were on the other side. But whatever we did had to be done with extreme caution.

We did not have a plan just yet but I thought it might be a good time to see what the Coroner was up to under the pretense of an interview. There was also a possibility that she had made a breakthrough in her forensic analysis of the murders. I did not tell the boys that I had ulterior motives and I felt a little guilty for failing to give full disclosure as we drove to the Medical Examiner's Offices and I asked them to wait in the car for me.

CHAPTER EIGHTEEN

●-●-●-·-●-●-●

I found her sorting through some papers and stuffing some into a briefcase that was atop her mahogany desk. She then walked behind her desk and picked up her jacket that was hanging on the chair and folded it onto her left elbow.

"Jack Chidi, you either have a good sense of timing or you are stalking me," she said with a smile as I walked towards her.

She wore a black skirt that just touched the top of her knees, hugging her hips, and a pink top with a low neckline that left her neck tantalisingly exposed. Her hair was braided and then coiled into a bun and held in place by a wooden hair pin that made her look as if she had a chopstick impaled into her skull.

She reached inside her desk drawer for her handbag, which she hoisted over her right shoulder effortlessly before rummaging for a set of keys. She then turned to face me with a shrug of her shoulders and said, "Well?"

"I thought I would come by and, eh, see what you were up to. I wanted to see you and talk about your work … I mean my work; you know the work that I do…"

Damn! Why was I so awkward with women? Okay, stop it Chidi, I told myself. Just cough and think of something clever to say. I should not have come here at all, bad idea!

"Chidi, Chidi, Chidi," she admonished me, letting each syllable roll out of her tongue softly.

She took two steps towards me and my eyes fell on her chest momentarily. I looked away quickly, pretending not to have seen a thing. My knees buckled and I slumped over slightly but I held ground. I must have looked really pathetic or really comical for she burst out laughing at my antics, not knowing there was no acting on my part, but I decided to ride the wave, and play it out. I grabbed my right knee with my right hand and did a little shimmy dance, with my behind waving in the air.

I danced to an imaginary song and then did a little Michael Jackson spin. I had not planned this out well and my lack of timing threw me off balance, sending me careening to the desk, narrowly missing her as I hit the front of her desk and held myself together awkwardly.

"Don't let my journalism fool you now," I said, straightening out. "I used to 'shake leg' back in the day!"

She was beside herself with laughter.

"You are really terrible, but cute!" she said and then beckoned me to walk out with her. "So, Mr. Dancer, what did you want to talk to me about? Is it something we can do over a drink or do you want to come back another time?"

I could not believe what I was hearing. Lowering my voice and putting on as serious a face as I could muster, I said:

"Well, I could come another time but I have a serious aversion to leaving until tomorrow what you can do today."

She bumped me playfully with her hips and smiled. It felt good. I had not touched a woman's hips in a long time. And not just any hips, I qualified as I felt myself coming alive.

"Oh, so what you are saying is that you don't have patience?" she mocked.

"I'm just saying that there is nothing wrong with today."

Despite my clumsy start, this was going well. I had completely forgotten that I had company waiting outside but they were all standing outside the car. I contemplated introducing them but I thought the better of it. Next time, I said to myself wryly.

"We can drive over in my friend's car or I can ride with you," I said to her as she locked up.

She smiled at me, motioned that I should join her, and then waved me along.

"Let me say bye to my posse and then we can see about that drink."

I ran to the car where Jacob, Otieno and Mburu were staring at Rosa, wide-eyed. They were curious but I did not have the time to explain, I told them that she had invited me for a drink and that she just might update me on her findings.

"I'll call you later," I said and walked back to where Rosa was waiting.

We walked to her car, a Peugeot 505. I could not believe that I was here with her, going for a drink. A few hours ago, I was dodging bullets and now, I was driving with the most beautiful woman I had ever had the pleasure to sit next to. And we were going for a drink! *Just the two of us, building castles in the sky, just the two us,* I hummed mentally, and off key!

"I hope you don't mind if I dash home for a quick shower and a change of attire - a shower for me of course!"

She was not really asking and I had no objections whatsoever. I was elated.

She lived in a three bedroom bungalow in Lavington, one of the coveted neighbourhoods in the city. She pulled her car in the garage and we got out. I followed her as she walked to and opened a side door that opened into her kitchen. It was nondescript but the layout was neat - almost too neat. Cooking utensils sat in a porcelain holder while pots and pans hang from a circular kitchen rack, arranged by size. They looked like huge chimes but they added a rustic look to an otherwise modern design. A basket holding an assortment of tropical fruits sat invitingly on the granite counter. I followed her into the living room and sat down on a beige micro-fiber couch that contoured and hugged me as I sank comfortably into it.

"Can I get you a drink?" she offered.

I stood up and walked over to where she was standing - next to a drinks cabinet that was carved into the wall. She had some liquor and several wine bottles and she poured herself a finger of Johnny

Walker. I was not really heavy on liquors or wine but I was not sure if I should ask for a beer. As if reading my mind, she told me to grab a cold beer in the fridge if that was what I preferred. She downed her drink with a quick tilt of her head, grabbed her handbag and headed upstairs to shower.

I walked into the kitchen and opened the fridge. It was fully stocked with vegetables, a small pot with leftovers, yoghurt and fruit drinks. On the side rack, I spotted some Tusker beers and I pulled one out. I needed an opener but I was not about to go through her cabinets to find one lest someone thought I was snooping. I took another tusker bottle and with my right hand, inverted it over the bottle on my left, locking the tops. Using the bridge of my thumb and forefinger as a fulcrum, I pulled the top bottle down with my right hand and popped the bottom one open. It was an old beer drinker's survival trick that you learned early.

I then went back to the couch and sat down. I could hear water running somewhere upstairs. It then hit me that she was upstairs, naked with water running all over her. I took a long gulp of my beer, trying to distract my mind from its sensual imaginings. Then I looked around her living room.

There was a huge abstract painting of a woman hanging from one wall. Next to it were some of her graduation photos from Loreto Convent, Msongari in Nairobi and another from Chienti Medical School in Italy. She was just as beautiful then as she was now. There were several photos of places she had visited - the shrine of St. Catherine of Siena and another taken in front of St. Peters Basilica. On the adjacent wall were several black and white photographs of her family, framed and arranged like a mosaic.

I walked over and looked at them more closely. One was that of her father, Roberto. Next to him was the photo of a woman who I presumed was her mother. 'Now I know where Rosa got her good looks from,' I smiled to myself. Below these were several photos taken at various stages in life. There were family portraits of the Alessandros celebrating love and happiness.

These reminded me that I did not have any photos of my father and I together and even worse, the memories I had of him were sad and distant. But I often wondered if photographs, frozen moments in time, really brought one joy or sadness over time and lives lost.

"Oh, I see you have met my family."

I turned around quickly to see her standing across the room. Rosa had startled me but I tried to play it off.

She was wearing a white sleeveless top, which showed off toned long arms, and a flowing dress that seemed to float behind her as she walked towards me. Her hair was now in a long pony tail and it swung gently from side to side as she walked and then calmed down as she stood by me and pointed to the photos. She touched each one gently, feeling their faces with her fingers on the glass. She seemed to lose herself in the memory of her loved ones, especially her parents.

"This is my mother," she said of the woman in the photo I had seen earlier. "My grandparents, Zenawi and Asefa, migrated here from Ethiopia after my mother was born."

She stopped for a minute as if a terrible thought had clutched her heart. She pointed to her father and I could see tears welling in her eyes even before she spoke. I put my hand in hers to tell her it was okay. Just to reassure her that I identified with her and I knew the loss and how profound it was. I empathetically told her about my father. She listened, all the while staring at her own father as if remembering him in my story. I was not sure who was helping whom here - just two souls trying to make meaning from loss.

"How did his death make you feel?" she asked somberly.

I looked at her. Her face had registered a hurt that I instantly recognised. I had seen it in my mother many times before.

"It was strange at first, not knowing him and being too young to understand what had really happened," I said sadly. "In a way, my father had died long before his physical death."

"What do you mean?" Rosa asked.

"I don't know, but the drinking and petty thefts were completely against his character. He was a proud man. Death, like poverty, is cruel," I said, amazed at how much I had internalised my father's pain.

"Death itself is not cruel. Those who perpetuate it are," Rosa said bitterly after I was done.

I sensed a deep seated anger in her voice and I wanted to say something to take away her pain but I could not think of anything that could mollify that.

"I agree that anyone who takes another's life is cruel but we must allow ourselves the capacity to forgive those who have done us wrong. Otherwise we live in that cesspool of bitterness and anger."

"Is that what you did, Jack?" she asked softly.

"Yes, I learned to forgive so that I could live," I answered.

She was quiet for a minute. It was as if she was wrestling with her own demons. I took another sip of my Tusker, savouring the hops that danced on my tongue with that unmistakable taste of a well-brewed lager.

"Death is inevitable. It is part of living," she said almost in a whisper, like one who had just resigned herself to fate.

"Does it bother you?"

"What?"

"Your work."

"Why would it bother me? There is dignity in forensic pathology."

She looked at me and smiled. Up until now I had forgotten that she was the Coroner and that murder had brought us together in the first place.

All evening she had been a woman, a beautiful woman who had captured my imagination and my fancy. Her graceful presence had thrown my investigative story out of the window for now and I visually embraced her comeliness with awe.

She brushed by me as she walked towards the kitchen and I followed. I watched as her hips buoyed in the long dress, swaying enchantingly with that gentle stride that made her look like she was gliding: seamless and seductive. The pied piper had nothing on Rosa, I thought ingeniously.

"You look nice!" I said, mesmerised.

Then I sat on a stool facing her. She smiled her thank you and opened the fridge. She peered into it and asked me if I wanted something to snack on. I was not exactly hungry but I was not about to turn down a chance to dine with her.

"Sure. What do you have?" I asked, not that it mattered – anything she offered would be like manna from heaven.

"We can make some chicken nuggets and sweet potato wedges if you don't mind getting your hands dirty."

"I'll have you know that I am a good chef."

"Really? You don't look like the type."

"When you live by yourself, you learn a thing or two about culinary matters. In fact, I'll do the chicken if you do the wedges and then we can judge each other's abilities based on taste and presentation."

She looked at me as if to gauge if I was serious or just facetious.

It turned out to be a nice meal after all and my chicken came out okay. I opened another beer while she fixed herself a margarita. Over dinner we had talked as if we had known each other for years. Conversation came easy and at times boisterously loud. We laughed often and playfully.

"So, are you domesticated or liberated?" she asked as I scrubbed the pan long after dinner. She was leaning on the counter with another margarita in hand.

"I am what we call a 'modernathal'."

"A who?"

"A 'modernathal' is a cross between Neanderthal man and Modern man," I explained with such certainty that it surprised me as well.

She burst out laughing; spraying the sip of margarita she had just taken all over the counter. It created a mist that obscured her from view for a second. Next thing I knew, she was on the floor writhing with laughter. I went over to help her up, offering her my hand. She tried placing her right hand into mine but the laughter was making it hard to coordinate. She was completely tickled and I could not get her to stop laughing. So I got down on my knees behind her and, placing my arms around and under her armpits, I pulled her up.

As we came to our feet, our body contours connected and synced like dancers in a choreographed waltz. A mild trace of sweet smelling perfume jostled my nostrils and her hair brushed gently against my face. I felt myself awaken, gently at first and then with that aching want that comes with an incessant pulsation. Her laughter had subsided and her eyes softened as she looked up at me. She clasped her hands into mine and ever so slightly gave me a squeeze and I knew that she could feel me, all of me but I did not care! I moved my arms around her waist and pulled her closer into me. I wanted to kiss her lips but I waited, knowing that there was no need to rush the moment. I closed my eyes and just held her, my head buried in her neck.

"So, modernathal," she started, pushing me gently away from her, but still holding my arms. "What is it that you want from me?" Her eyes dropped to my chest and then came up to meet mine.

I was not sure what the question was referencing, so I hesitated. She pulled herself away from me, picked up her drink and walked to the living room, sat down on the couch and crossed her legs.

"Well, I could …I would like to…I wanted to interview you for the paper, you know, an interview for work…." I was stumbling all over instead of simply telling her that I had been thinking about her, and that I wanted to be with her.

"And here I am thinking that you were going to ask about something else," she said, looking right into me. I swallowed.

"I mean about forensics," she added as if it was an afterthought. she uncrossed her legs and asked me to join her.

I did not feel like discussing the murders, not now. Not after what we had just shared in the kitchen, and definitely not now I thought as I sat down beside her.

"Well, we can talk about that if that is okay with you. I am a journalist but I sometimes leave work at home."

Good come back, though maybe a mite too late!

"I'm glad to hear that. Like you, I leave my work at the office. It would be kind of crazy for me to bring my work home, eh?" She smiled.

I tried to change the subject back to ourselves. I had to be tactful and not push her away by my neediness but I wanted to be with her, to spend some time in her presence and perhaps feel her body next to mine. It was as if something magical was happening but I did not quite know how to read it or how to act on it.

There was no need to rush things and it was a good idea to quit while I was ahead. It was time for me to leave, I thought to myself. I could still catch a bus home. I looked at the time. Half past ten. Still early though, but I did not want to be walking in Dagoretti after midnight. In the presence of Rosa and the peaceful quiet of suburbia, I had forgotten about the chaotic existence and danger that was my world.

"I hope I can see you again, for an interview of course, and then perhaps after we can go out for a drink."

She smiled. I gulped down my beer, desperately hoping that she would ask me to stay but she did not. I stood up and made to shake her hand goodbye but she got up from her seat and gave me a hug.

"I would ask you to stay but it might be a little too soon," she confessed, to my delight.

I wanted to protest but being in her embrace had me in a loop, tongue-tied and confused. Her body felt so nice and I was sure she felt the same way too but she did not change her mind about my staying.

"I'll drive you to the bus station," she offered but it was not what I had hoped for so I declined politely.

She pecked me on the right cheek, a peck that lingered long after my short walk to the station and my bus ride to town.

I did not think it was a good idea to go home - not by myself anyway so that night I hid out at Mburu's house in Kibera.

Rosa Alessandro. I thought about her all night. I replayed the events of the day in my mind. My mind refused to dwell on the gunfight earlier or the encounter with Fatima and kept coming back to Rosa. She seduced me to sleep.

CHAPTER NINETEEN

● ● ● · ● ●

I woke up early the next day. Mburu had already left without a note. I fetched a glass of water and sat down by the small kitchen table. I had to find a way to make sense of all the information I had, to see if I had enough to write a story that could withstand legal challenges. Was I reading too much in to Wagateru's death or was it really related to the serial killings? The thought reminded me that Meredith had not called me. I grabbed my phone and dialed the New London Grills number. The phone rang and then went to voice mail. I looked at the time. It was too early, they were not open yet. I would call back later.

Despite not getting in touch with Meredith, I felt happy with myself, somehow. I knew that had to do with Rosa, and also the fact that I was getting close to tying all the pieces of the city murders together. I needed one more push to tip things over; just a piece of evidence that would place Kamau Kariuki at the crime scene. Everything pointed to him: all the murder victims, except Wagateru, had paid him exorbitant sums of money before they died. That much we knew. But why kill them if they were making down payments for a house in KenView? That did not make sense to me. And if he was the serial murderer how did he do it?

Yes, why and how: that's all that I needed to know to nail him or the sick bastard behind this bullshit. Kamau Kariuki was the why, and he was going down. And for sleeping with Fatima, he was a 'goner' anyway. If Ali had had it for me for dating his sister, Kamau, sleeping with his wife was a dead man walking! The only thing we needed now, I thought to myself, was a break before it came to that.

Rosa Alessandro. She came back to me like lightning. I had enjoyed my time with her so much so that I had all but forgotten about the investigations; and even when the subject came up, I had not felt compelled to delve into it. But who would have wanted to talk death with so much life around? Besides, I was sure she would have told Ali if she had found something.

I had shown poor judgment - taking the bus from her house and that late in the evening. I should have left earlier, or stayed with her. Even though I had changed routine and come to Mburu's, it was still not a good idea to travel alone and in the open when I knew the man in black and his team of thugs were prowling around for my blood.

I had to stay sharp, vigilant and alive. With Mburu out on some errand, I did not feel safe to venture out on my own. I stayed indoors with curtains closed and the door locked. It did not take me long to coax myself back to sleep. I needed it.

Mburu woke me up at about three o'clock in the afternoon. I had slept intermittently throughout the day but I felt well rested - and hungry. After a quick wash, we went to a nearby kiosk and ordered some *chapati* and collard greens mixed with spinach. Mburu assured me that the owner, a little lady with quick hands, could be trusted with her cooking.

"So, what do you have planned today? I know you are up to something," Mburu stated.

He was right. I was toying with the idea of visiting with Rosa again. I had thoroughly enjoyed my evening with her. I was even beginning to think that perhaps there might be something there but I did not want to seem too pushy or smitten, but surely, seeing her again would be nice. Meredith crossed my mind; she was more up my alley than Rosa but how could I resist that magical pull, especially how I felt with her in my arms? But should I not be thinking about staying alive instead of my amorous life? It was confusing, with all things coming to me at once: I needed clarity of thought.

Ali must have much more information than we had but he had closed the option of my calling him for an update - and I was not going to be the first to tell him about his wife. That was the mother of betrayals: his wife and his prime suspect having an affair.

Ali and I may have had our differences here and there but when all was said and done, we were still friends. How does one broach such a subject, would he believe me anyway even if I was to tell him? I knew sooner or later he would find out about it and the ones to suffer the most would be the children - if things went south, but somehow I talked myself into believing that it was best left alone. Whatever her reasons, no doubt Fatima had not thought it through when she made her choice to cheat on her husband.

We walked back to Mburu's apartment. Somehow, I felt safe in Kibera. I was sure that it had something to do with 'Lucy', but also perhaps, it was the protective anonymity provided by all the people milling around me, in one of the largest slums in Nairobi.

A mini-van loaded with tourists, their white faces peering intently out of the windows, their doors locked tight, nearly forced us into an open sewer. Children ran beside the van, asking for candy and dollar bills. The white faces obliged by throwing cookies and half-eaten sandwiches like visitors feeding animals at the zoo. Some confectionary landed on the muddy and unsanitary roadside and as the children scrambled for it the cameras clicked away.

"So, what do you think of Kibera?" Mburu interrupted my flow of thoughts.

This was not my first time in the slums, so I figured he was just making conversation prompted by the unseemly sight of cameras on needy children.

"Well, poverty is the same everywhere you go. The smells, the cries, the decay is all the same whether you are here, Asia, South Africa, America or Europe."

"Yeah, man, poverty stinks but in that stench there is the smell of real life. I just can't stand to see these tourist buggers coming to photograph us for sport as if we are a new species. I guess animal photography in the parks has lost its appeal."

I could not agree with him more. I remembered that tourist at the Waldoria calling the manager, 'boy' to his face.

At about four thirty that evening, Jacob and Otieno picked us up and we all drove to my apartment. I needed a change of clothes.

Otieno complained that I had not answered his calls but he would forgive me once I gave him the juicy details of my night with Rosa. I could see disappointment on his face when I told him that nothing happened; we had just talked, had dinner and after a few beers I had taken a bus to Mburu's house.

"So, she invites you to her place and you sit there talking? She literally throws herself at you and you take a bus home? What the fuck?" He looked at me incredulously.

"Dude, I will see her again. You can't just assume that she wanted to do me just because she invited me to her house."

"What does it mean when a woman asks a man to her house for a drink?" Otieno asked, waving his hands, looking for support from Mburu and Jacob. "What does it mean?"

"The problem with you," Mburu said, laughing and pointing at Otieno, "is that you don't understand women. She just wanted to spend some time with the guy. What's wrong with that?"

"They could have gone to any place between here and the moon to have a drink but she chose her house. Why else would she do that?"

Jacob, who usually stayed out of our heated exchanges, chimed in.

"It means nothing," he said. "She probably likes him but not the way Otieno might think. There are different kinds of women. Some just want a good time, others just a friend and still others want something wholesome and worthy of their time."

We all looked at him. It was the longest utterance Jacob had ever made with such profundity.

The laughter and the philosophy suddenly stopped. The door of my apartment was ajar. Mburu quickly pulled out his gun, cocked it and walked past me. I ducked down and followed. At the door, Mburu paused for a few seconds, listening. Without as much as a word, he kicked the door wide open with his right leg, jumped in and dropped on one knee. He pointed the gun to the left towards my living room, and then to the kitchen. I braced myself for another firefight but there was nothing.

My heart was pounding loudly. I could hear it. The veins on my forehead throbbed. Otieno was walking behind me with his hands outstretched, tagging at my shirt. My living room was in shambles, papers strewn everywhere and my couch had been turned upside down.

Mburu got up from his crouched position and walked stealthily towards the bedroom. I crawled towards the kitchen to get a knife. The cabinets had been ransacked, as if someone had been looking for something in a hurry. I grabbed the knife I found on the floor by the fridge and followed Mburu into the bedroom. We checked under the bed, the closet, everywhere, and found no one.

The police came two hours later, someone must have called them - they recorded statements, dusted for prints and asked about missing items. I had not taken an inventory but as far as I could tell there was nothing missing.

I packed some work clothes into a suitcase and we drove off. Otieno invited me to stay at his place but I did not want to jeopardise his family - I also did not feel safe in Dagoretti anymore. I was a walking target and unless Ali or I stopped these bastards, it was not going to end well.

After driving in silence, Mburu burst out with yet another philosophical quip: life was too precious to be lived in silence and he offered us all a drink. He was also trying to enjoy his vacation, he added. Nobody objected.

He opted for the Hotel Geneva off Lenana Road, where he told us security was tight.

We sat on the terrace facing the gardens where tourists, perhaps the same ones that we had seen in Kibera, were busy sampling the cuisine of wild game and other niceties as their children frolicked about and screamed in play. Waiters and waitresses in black uniforms milled around them, but no camera clicked. Perhaps pleasure was not as photogenic as poverty, Mburu observed. Or as dramatic, I added.

I was glad we had decided to sit outside in the open. The soft Nairobi breeze and the airy scenery of luxurious living was a far cry from the shambles of my Dagoretti digs.

As soon as our drinks came, I quickly took a huge swig from my Tusker bottle, and let out a soft belch that hit my nostrils, awakening my senses. I felt the cold beer settle into the pit of my stomach. I pulled on my cigarette and sat back, letting the smoke drift from my nostrils and into the evening light. With every sip, I felt my muscles relax, and by the time I was on my third beer, I was all but my old self again.

I called Meredith yet again. Someone picked up the phone and I felt relief mixed with apprehension as I stepped away from the noisy table. But there was silence on the other end. I was not sure that they had heard me so I again asked to speak with Meredith.

"She's not here at the moment. Can I take a message?" a voice answered.

"Did she come in today or is she not available?"

"She's not in. Do you want to leave a message?"

"Leave a message, why can't I just talk to her?" I was getting testy. Then I remembered Ben, the manager. "Hey, let me speak to Ben."

I paced up and down the patio, waiting for Ben.

"Hello. Ben speaking, how may I help you?"

"Hey, Ben, this is Jack Chidi of *The Daily Grind*. I'm Meredith's friend."

"Hey, Jack, how are you?"

"I have been trying to get in touch with Meredith. Do you know where she is?"

After some agonising seconds, he told me what I did not want to hear: she had not come in to work, two nights in a row.

"Did she call in sick?" I asked, hoping to hear that she had come down with something.

"No. She left here in a hurry, the night before last, after talking with some two men."

"What men?"

"Just some two guys in suits," he answered nonchalantly.

My heart leapt to my throat. No, it could not be! Wagateru had been visited by some men in suits and now Meredith. Jesus Christ! I remembered the veiled threat but Ben had no more details. I thanked him and went and sat down. There had to be another explanation. Maybe a relative had died or something and she was needed back in Nyeri.

My beer tasted like crap and I did not want to drink anymore. I sat down wondering what the best course of action was. Surely, I had to let someone know that she was in trouble.

Mburu excused himself. After a while he came back and asked a waiter to add two chairs to our table.

"What for - what are the chairs for?" Otieno wanted to know.

"I just asked some girls to join us for a drink, that's all," Mburu sat back and smiled at Otieno who looked as if he could not believe the magic would work. "If I'm going out, I'm going out my way and in style. I might as well die loving."

I did not care one way or the other. No, I could not stand it; the girls would only serve to remind me of Meredith. I felt sick in the stomach at the very thought that she might have met Wagateru's fate. Then it became more than just a feeling. If I stayed here longer, I was going to throw up.

I stood up and walked inside to look for the bathroom. My mind was running through all kinds of scenarios. I hated that I knew so little about Meredith, her contacts, her friends, her relatives. I squeezed through a multitude of people standing by the bar watching a soccer game. Arsenal was taking on Manchester United and the patrons, some wearing their team's jerseys, cheered them on. I edged my way slowly, my shoulder tilted to one side to ease my way through the crowd. Fighting to get through did not add to my cheer but I made it to the bathroom.

The fumes from the air-freshener were quite harsh but so was the strong acrid smell of urine. Just as I finished peeing, I felt the tingly feeling in my jaws and I leaned over the urinal, with my right hand bracing me against the front wall. I convulsed once, feeling the sharp, painful jerking of my guts being ripped out. I braced myself for a second one but nothing. I tasted bile in my tongue and I spat it out before I surrendered everything I had in my stomach.

Then I washed my hands and looked at my face in the mirror. I had not looked at myself in days. Save for the circles under my eyes and some redness in them, I was not in such a terrible shape for one who had gone through so much in a short period of time. Hell, I had just thrown up. I splashed cold water on my face, wiped myself dry and walked out.

On my way back, I stopped at the bar. Manchester United and Arsenal were still tied. The crowd was tighter and I did not feel like squeezing through cheering fans - some of whom had taken to loudly coaching their respective teams and players on how best to score. I turned back and walked through the dining lounge on the mezzanine floor, around the back of the bar and towards the patio.

And then, suddenly, I saw her. I stopped in my tracks.

Rosa was sitting at a table, with a man. David Kantar. I instantly recognised him - the famous chairman of the East African Bank, the largest investment bank in the country.

I thought I should walk over and say hello but I realised that I was trembling. She looked so beautiful in a red, strapless evening dress. Her hair was flowing over her shoulders and with some strands fluttering gently in the breeze. When she laughed, she threw her head back ever so slightly, making her hair dance in the light. She cut into the backdrop, the Nairobi skyline, like a piece of live art. Her bare shoulders, inviting, but I remained immobilised, peering from behind a pillar like a tardy schoolboy.

I looked at her again. She was saying something to him as she reached over and placed her hand on his. Damn! That should be me, right there, next to her, I said to myself. That is, if I had called her earlier in the day like I had wanted to or better, if I had made plans last night just before I left. I do not know why I was so agitated. She had promised absolutely nothing to me. Besides, Kantar could have been just a friend. But what the fuck were they doing here, together anyway?

He was a known philanthropist who spent a great deal of time lobbying the government to invest more in the youth of the country. He had been appointed to head the Youth Empowerment Commission and in his first year, he had seen the opening of the Business Apprenticeship Initiative (BAI) which gave companies subsidies to employ and train youth in various business skills. After a two year stint, those young men and women who were interested in starting their own businesses were given small loans, and then mentored through a partnership of banking officials and members of the business community.

BAI offices were opened in several city centers around the country with very promising results. Mr. Kantar had been featured in several local and international magazines and appeared in all major TV and Radio stations. CNN, BBC and VOA all wanted a piece of him while several African countries sought his expertise to help them model similar initiatives in their countries. Two America multi-national corporations who were trying to penetrate the East African Market tried to hire him as a consultant but he politely declined these lucrative offers, saying that his heart was in shaping the leaders of tomorrow.

So, try as I could, I was not able to hate him, except for a vague general resentment: why did the rich get all the good things in life?

Still, I blamed myself for not having asked Rosa out. "Better to have tried and failed than not to have tried at all," I told myself. I had done the same dilly-dallying with Meredith, who I may have lost too. I had to be bolder if ever I got another chance.

For now, I thought, the prudent thing to do was to just go over and say hello. There was no law against that. It was then that I realised that I was beginning to sweat out of physical and mental distress. It did not have to be this way!

I hurried back the same way I had come; through the dining room, back to the bar and inched my way through the cheering patrons and finally back to where my friends were sitting, talking excitedly about the two college girls who had refused to join our table.

I sat down quickly and gulped down my drink.

"Man, are we thirsty today or what…" Otieno started to say but I did not let him finish.

"I just saw Rosa," I blurted out.

"So what?" he said with gritted teeth, jerking his head in the direction of the two girls as if to tell me to shut up.

"She's with another dude!"

"What the hell are you…? Oh my God, Chidi, I knew it!" Otieno exploded. "You are into her. Look at you man, you are jealous!"

I looked sharply at him, trying to stare him into silence but he was relentless.

"Guys, look at this shit, man. What the hell? You go falling in love with everyone…."

"Shut up, man. I'm not jealous. I don't even know her," I protested weakly.

"The other day it was Meredith, now it's the Coroner…or Rosa as you would have us say!"

"Leave the man alone," Mburu said sternly.

It felt good for someone else to speak on my behalf. I reached for another Tusker and poured myself another drink. My hands were shaking and I began to hate myself for betraying my feelings.

I could have just walked over and asked her to join us for a drink after her meeting with Mr. Kantar. 'Surely there was nothing wrong with that,' I told myself unconvincingly. I looked in their direction and caught a glimpse of Mr. Kantar talking to a waiter. It looked like he was paying their bill and my heart fell to the floor. They were leaving before I even had the courage to go say hello.

"I think they are leaving," I said more to myself.

"I have never seen you so smitten," Mburu said and suddenly stood up adjusting his pants. "I have to see this woman up close."

He stood up and begun to walk over in their direction.

Otieno too got up and followed suit. Jacob and I stayed behind, sitting in silence. The problem with jealousy was that there is no known cure for it and I had never thought myself the type to be inflicted with this scourge! I had taken temporary vows of celibacy and they had lasted me these many months, so why this thing now?

After a while, Otieno came back, alone, and sat down.

"Dude, I'm sorry man, but they could just be friends. You can still get her."

His words were neither encouraging nor chastising but they did not make me feel any better.

"Hey, where's Mburu?" Jacob asked Otieno.

"He went to the boys' room," he answered and then looked in the direction of the college girls to find that they had found other company.

He shrugged his shoulders and grabbed his beer.

"And that's all, folks!" he said resignedly, pointing to the girls.

We sat there silently for a while. I looked over to where Rosa had been sitting with Kantar but they had left. I tried to peer through the crowds to catch a last glimpse of her but to no avail. I felt a huge knot form in my stomach. It then inched its way to my throat. The feeling of sadness mixed with self-loathing became that of sickness and loss.

Just then Mburu came charging through the crowds. He seemed agitated and I thought that he too had had to push his way through the rowdy soccer fans at the bar.

"We have to go, now!" he urged us.

I sat up, staring at Mburu. He had that same look I had seen before the gunfight.

"Why? What's wrong?" Otieno asked.

"Don't argue with me on this one. We must leave right away!"

"What the fuck, man. What's going on?" I asked.

"The man in black is here!" he said, trying to be as calm as possible without sounding alarmed.

CHAPTER TWENTY

• • • · • • •

I shot up to my feet. Jacob hurried off, keys in hand, saying he would bring the car to the front.

We did not have the bill so Mburu dropped a thousand shillings note on the table. I pulled out a few hundred shillings and added to his amount and we filed out behind him. The crowds at the bar were louder than before: the game had ended in a draw and there would be overtime play set to start shortly. The fans dispensed their post-game analysis to anyone who would care to listen.

As I inched through the chaos, I looked up and saw Rosa walking towards the exit with Kantar following closely behind. He had his left hand on her lower back and she did not seem to mind at all. Some business meeting!

That now familiar pang of jealous pain shot up again and settled in the pit of my stomach. There she was, with another man, walking as if she owed the world nothing.

A Toyota Avalon pulled up and the valet jumped out. Kantar opened the door for her. He closed it after she had slipped in, gave the valet a tip and walked over to the driver's side and drove off.

"Mburu, what's going on, man?" I asked as we waited for Jacob to bring our car. "Do you think he followed us here again?" I was panicking.

He looked around without saying anything. Just then he ducked his head slightly, and simultaneously thrust his right hand into his left breast pocket and I knew he was going for 'Lucy.' His eyes had locked on someone. I followed his gaze to the entrance and that is when I saw him: the man in black. It was one thing to hear someone tell you that the bastard trying to kill you is around - it is another to see him for yourself. But he was also leaving, it seemed.

He walked hurriedly as if he was late for something. I saw him skip-run across to the parking and jump into a black Range Rover. As he sped past the hotel entrance, I saw the shattered back window. There was no mistaking him!

We stepped out just as Jacob came squealing round the bend. We quickly hopped in and drove off after him.

"Follow him," Mburu told Jacob, pointing to the tail lights in the distance and fading fast. Jacob stepped on it and the engine roared. The last time he was torturing the engine like this we were being chased. This time we were on the giving end - not much consolation but it felt better this way.

Mburu pulled out 'Lucy' and checked the clip for bullets. Satisfied, he put it back and cocked the gun. It still scared me to have a gun so close at hand but at the same time it was a good thing to see. Jacob sped down the narrow strip of road leading out of the Hotel Geneva. The headlights split the darkness. As we rounded a little corner past the hill leading back onto Lenana Road, we started gaining on the Range Rover.

"Slow down, Jacob, but make sure we don't lose them. We are going to get some mother-fucking answers tonight," Mburu said, sounding so much in control.

I felt strangely calm but I knew I was scared as hell.

"Could someone please tell me what is going on?" Jacob asked loudly.

Otieno, who had not spoken a word, explained. His crackling voice gave away the excitement he was trying to conceal. After he was done, Jacob let out a muted curse. I had never heard him curse before. He did not say another word but his eyes kept darting at the driving mirror. He pulled his seat forward, adjusting his position like one digging in for the long haul.

The Range Rover joined the four lane highway leading out of the city; we followed, keeping several cars between us and at a safe distance. I wondered if the driver knew he was being followed but there was nothing in his driving to suggest that he was running - the Range Rover could have easily outpaced us if he had wanted to; they had done it before. We had him and the element of surprise was on our side.

At the junction into State House Road, the Range Rover veered right onto Old Kings Highway and took another right into Lumumba Avenue and then onto Embakasi Road. And we followed.

After a short drive the Range Rover pulled into a driveway leading up to the Hartford Motel, off Kimote Boulevard. The cars between us and the Range Rover did not follow in so we had to drive past or risk being exposed. We turned into the next driveway, a used car sales lot, where Jacob pulled into one of the empty parking spots and turned off the headlights.

"Guys, this is it. Let's find a way to the motel, quietly. Follow me!" Mburu whispered and then, gun in hand, opened his door, stepped out, and quietly pushed his door shut.

He then squatted, keeping his torso low and ran between the used cars towards a small building behind the lot and then towards the motel we had just passed. We slipped out of the car and followed suit.

From there, we could see the motel clearly. It was a long two storied structure with a set of iron steps going up to the second floor on each side which gave it a U-shaped appearance. The entrance was complete with dimly lit blinking neon lights that greeted your arrival. Mburu squeezed himself between some thick bushes, trying to get through, but there was a chain link fence running through the bushes. I walked parallel with the fence, trying to find a way in. There was none.

It was either climbing over or creeping under. I grabbed the bottom hexagons of the fence and yanked it. It made a jiggling sound that stopped me in my tracks. No need to announce ourselves. I whispered to Otieno for help. Together we pulled gently, and as the fence grew taut, we pulled harder, the fence gave way slowly as the undergrowth that had twined itself on it got uprooted and broke off. Mburu, crawled under, followed by Jacob and Otieno. I was the last one in and we huddled behind some shrubbery fronting the motel parking lot.

We scoured for the Range Rover. The car park was not well lit, so it took us a little while to get used to the darkness and make out what was in front of us.

"There!" Jacob whispered, excitedly pointing towards the far side of the motel. The Range Rover was parked under a tree away from the other cars in the lot, facing the entrance of the motel. I was not sure that the man in black was still in it so we could not make a move just yet.

We did not wait long. A red glow inside the Range Rover flared and then quickly dimmed in the dark interior. We knew at once that he was in there smoking a cigarette. What or who was he waiting for?

Just then, the front door of the motel opened and I saw Kantar walk out, alone. What the hell was he doing? He continued walking towards the parking lot and after a while we saw headlights illuminate the area and the Toyota Avalon came to full view. I looked over at the Range Rover, there was no movement there and my eyes darted back to the Avalon. Kantar got in, started the car and pulled up and parked in front of the motel - at the far end. He got out, casually and walked around the car and opened the passenger door.

Rosa stepped out and I saw her place her hand onto his outstretched arm and as they walked towards one of the motel rooms I heard then laughing. They stopped momentarily, for him to open the door, and just as she walked in, he placed his right hand between her legs. She slapped it away playfully as she went in, and he, taking one last look outside closed the door behind them.

Kantar's move begun to make sense: he had left Rosa in the car, fetched the keys to the room, and came back for her so they could enter discreetly. 'That could have been me,' I said to myself.

And Bingo! It suddenly hit me! The man in black was here to get her. He had been following me, had placed us together in her house, and now, he was to make her and Kantar suffer the same fate as Wagateru and probably Meredith just because of me. I looked over at the Range Rover. He was still in there smoking. I do not know what it was about that the red glow from the cigarette that awakened the 'animal.' I started towards him. Mburu tagged at my hand, "Jack, chill, man!" I did not heed him.

I started walking slowly towards the Range Rover. He had the missing link - hell he was the link to all the bullshit and murders. No more games, no more shadowing, nooses, veiled threats, car chases, break-ins and gunfights; tonight it all ended, one way or the another - but he was not going to kill another innocent life. No, not again - it was all ending tonight!

Mburu joined me and together we walked stealthily behind the bushes to our right. We inched closer and closer until we were about ten feet behind the Range Rover. I could make out the outline of his head as he sat there smoking. The cigarette smell wafted past us and I crept up and knelt directly under the Range Rover. He had the radio on and was listening to some soft country music.

Mburu put his hand on my shoulder gently and I looked back. His face was so close to mine I could feel his breath. He pointed his fingers to his eyes and then to the shattered glass above. He then pointed to me and then to the driver's side. He took a deep breath and with his legs slightly apart for balance, he stood up, pointed the gun inside the car from the back and pulled the safety off. Click, click. The hammer was cocked!

"You better not move a muscle, asshole!" Mburu said to the man, slowly. His gun was trained to the back of his head. We had him.

I looked up. Mburu's hand was steady, pointing the gun inside the car. I crouched up and inched my way to the driver's side. I hoped that this is what Mburu had in mind.

"Put your hands on top of the steering wheel slowly," Mburu instructed, his voice cold and steely.

The man in black placed his hands on the wheel, one after the other. His eyes were trained on the driving mirror, trying to make out who was giving the orders.

I immediately pulled his door open with my left hand, stepped forward and with my right hand, grabbed him by the back of his head. Clearly, he had not expected this and as he turned to see what the hell was going on, I pulled his head right into my left elbow with a resounding thwack! Without letting up, I banged his head again with my elbow and as he brought his hands to his face for protection, I put all my weight on my left foot, pivoted and came up with a resounding left to the jaw. His head snapped backwards. I grabbed him with both hands, pulled him sharply towards me and head-butted him right across the temple. He was out but I continued to pummel him with my fists until Mburu pulled me off him. I let him go and he slumped onto the steering wheel and Mburu held him up before he could inadvertently blow the horn.

Otieno and Jacob now came to where we were.

"Damn, what the fuck did you do to him?" Otieno asked as we pulled him out and set him down behind the Range Rover.

Mburu was going through his pockets for weapons and identification. He pulled out the man's wallet from his back pocket and handed it to me. He then climbed in and rummaged through the car. In the glove box he pulled out a .38 revolver.

"Is he dead?" Jacob was asking.

"No, man, he's just out."

I looked at the man in black, lying on the pavement with his head to one side, blood trickling from his nostrils. He was not a big man, rather slim and his choice of black clothing really made him look thinner than he really was. For someone who had raised so much havoc, he now looked quite innocent and peaceful - almost harmless.

"We have to tie him up. I'll fetch a rope," said Jacob.

He crawled out and ran back towards the fence and into the used-car lot where we had parked. After a short while he came back with some nylon strings and we secured the man in black. I looked towards the motel. There was no indication that anyone had heard any commotion. I walked over to the driver's side where Mburu sat with one leg dangling outside. He was admiring the .38, perhaps contemplating replacing 'Lucy.' Using the panel lighting, I opened the wallet. From his National I.D card, a little frayed at the edges, we learnt that he was Nahashon Juma, one of the directors of KayKay Concepts. The man in black, the killer, was now tied directly to Kamau Kariuki.

Mburu looked at me without speaking and then motioned his head towards Nahashon. I did not know what he meant so I asked him.

"I can make him talk. It's going to get ugly, but he has to tell us everything he knows. The answers lie there," he said and pouted his lower lip towards Nahashon Juma.

I now understood what he was saying but I was not up for torture - it could extract truth as much as falsehood. And what could we do with it anyway?

"I am not up to it. Let's phone Ali," I suggested. "This is theirs, now."

"It's your call, man, but I can make him talk."

So what if he talked, I thought to myself. We did not have authority to make any arrests. We would still have to hand everything over to the police. Ali was our best bet. We would tell him everything and he would take it from here.

I was about to dial Ali's number when we saw a car pull up and park behind Kantar's car. The driver of this car sat there for a few minutes and after a little while, the door opened and he got out. From the physique I guessed it had to be a man. He stepped out quickly, walked and stood in front of the door to the room where Rosa and

Kantar were. He placed his ear to the door and listened, after which he pulled something from his pocket. He knelt in front of the door and begun to pick at the lock. I looked at Otieno incredulously. The man in black - Nahashon Juma - mumbled something, signaling that he was coming to. Otieno bent over and with lightning speed struck him once in the jaw and he was out cold, again.

"What in hell is going on?" I asked Mburu rhetorically because I knew he must have had the same thought: something really bad was about to happen and we were right in the middle of it. And we thought we had this under control?

I could not sit still any longer. I pulled my phone out again to call Ali and then realised that it would take him or the police too long to get here, by which time Rosa would be dead. The thought of someone hurting her was all I needed - I had to act and act now!

I crawled out from behind the car and ran cross the dark parking lot, ducking in behind cars until I reached the delivery bay to the right of the motel. I jumped off the platform to the unpaved patch of dirt below and in no time I was at the back end of the motel. Slowly, I walked across the row of motel rooms trying to find the one Rosa was in. I stopped at every window and listened for voices or any kind of commotion.

It was dark out back except for the dim lighting coming from a distant security light and so I had to feel my way around using the wall. Perhaps I could warn them that there was someone prying their door open. But how would I explain my presence behind their window? I thought of throwing some rocks and breaking their window panes. Or better still, alert the front desk clerk, maybe he could raise the alarm. Yes, the damn alarm! But the crouching crook would see me and perhaps start shooting before I got to the reception.

In the midst of indecision, I heard voices and giggling emanating from behind the window above me. I grabbed the ledge and, as quietly as I could, pulled myself up to the window and peered in through the corner of the lace curtains. I could not get a good angle from this position so I moved to the right corner, tilted my head and pushed my face right between the cold concrete wall and the ledge of the window.

The room was lit by a small bedside lamp. Kantar, undressed, lay on his back, watching Rosa. It was her turn, undressing, slowly, teasingly. She pulled off the straps of her dress over her slender shoulders, all the while moving her hips rhythmically and seductively. My jaw dropped and I momentarily forgot why I was here and watched as she moved like a hypnotic belly-dancer. Her hair fell over her shoulders and down her back, covering her neck like a mane. I felt things inside me begin to stir but I kept watching, transfixed.

Kantar, giddy with anticipation, was licking his lips and saying something to her. I could not make out what he was muttering but I was sure it did not involve the changing weather patterns. Finally, she snapped her bra and stood in front of him naked. He stretched out his hand towards her breasts but she pushed him back. He laughed and said something else to her. She got on the bed with him and straddled him. He closed his eyes and waited to be pleasured.

I was always dismissive of voyeurism but I felt myself drift away into an erotic whirlwind. I was watching intently, having forgotten that I was supposed to alert them of the imminent danger lurking at their front door, when suddenly someone touched me on my shoulder!

"What are you watching?" It was Mburu. "Let me see."

He had completely startled me.

"Man, you scared me to death!" I said shoving my elbow into his ribs, a little embarrassed. Mburu peered in unperturbed.

"Hello, mama!" Mburu whispered when he caught sight of a naked Rosa straddling Kantar.

I squeezed my face next to Mburu's on the window pane. Suddenly, I saw Kantar sit up, start to get up and, sit back down. And just then I saw the masked man enter the room - he had picked the lock! Rosa tried to cover her naked body with the bedcover.

"Hey, what do you want? Get out!" Kantar shouted, facing him.

Rosa, now covered, crawled out from the other side of the bed and began to collect her clothing.

"What do you want?" Kantar shouted at the figure that had just broken in. "You must leave right now!"

"Shut up! Shut your goddamn mouth!"

It was the man. He was wearing a knitted face mask. He looked menacing as he walked across the room pointing a gun at Kantar, who tried unsuccessfully to cover his now limp dick with the palm of his hand. He then started pleading for his life.

"If it's money, I have plenty in my wallet!" Kantar said, begging the gunman.

I could not make out what he said but I saw him motion Kantar to pick up his trousers and jacket.

Rosa was now dressed. I was sorry I was not much of a help but almost happy that the gunman was not paying her too much attention. Covering himself with a pillow, Kantar picked up his shirt and trousers, put them on, then took out his wallet and handed to the man what appeared to be some bills. The man grabbed them and threw them over his shoulders in disgust. He gave Kantar some instructions, pointing his gun at him with careless confidence. This was a robbery about to go bad.

Kantar now grabbed his jacket from the floor and pulled out a check book and began to scribble on it. He paused to ask a question to the man and then, his hands shaking visibly, he resumed writing, pausing ever so briefly to steady his hand by flexing his wrists as if to take the tension out of the joints.

He tore the check off and handed it to the gunman who looked it over thoroughly before he slid it into his pocket.

Kamau Kariuki! It had to be him. It made sense: with the help of his crime partner, they stalked wealthy couples, found them in compromising positions and blackmailed them with threats of violence and exposure, received the check and used KayKay Concepts as cover - a pretext that the victim was purchasing a house. It made sense.

But now, what about Rosa? What would the gunman do with her?

"We have to take him out," I whispered to Mburu.

The gunman said something to Rosa. She looked at him quickly and then half-ran towards the door where I lost her. Run! Rosa! Run! I wanted to scream. She did not make it to the door. A rough hand quickly pulled her back into the room

I must have made a noise for Mburu nudged me with his elbow. My gaze went back to Kantar and the gunman.

The crook took out what appeared to be a little box from his back pocket, opened it, took out a syringe fitted with a needle, and with one smooth move he braced Kantar by the neck with his left hand, rolled him over, trapped him between his legs and was struggling to inject the syringe into Kantar's carotid artery.

That was when Mburu jumped into action. He immediately broke the window with the butt of his gun and quickly pulled the curtains to the side. Just as the gunman, turned with his gun pointing towards the window Mburu shot him - he buckled and fell off the bed. Mr. Kantar scrambled from the bed, and ran towards the door, a shot rang out and he fell. The gunman was still alive.

Mburu opened fire again - two quick bursts and then ducked behind the window. I was now crouched into a ball. The gunman returned fire, hitting the window sill. I covered my head with my hands hoping that no bullet would pierce through the wall.

Mburu stood up again and emptied his clip. He then ducked down again just as the gunman responded with a staccato. Mburu re-loaded. I pulled out my phone to call Ali while we had the gunman trapped inside. There was no way we were going to let him escape.

It was then that we heard the sirens and saw the flashing blue lights. The police were here! Someone must have called them.

CHAPTER TWENTY ONE

● ● ● · ● ●

"Everybody, come out with your hands in the air!" A voice from a megaphone announced, "We have the place surrounded."

To the left and right of us, I saw flashlights - a dog barked and I knew the police were circling the building. Mburu stood up, holstered 'Lucy' and raised his hands in the air. I followed suit. Within a matter of seconds, we were handcuffed and frog-matched towards the front. A rough-looking constable talked on his walkie-talkie.

"Chief, we have them, and we have recovered a gun."

"Bring them up."

I tried to explain but no one was listening. We were brought up to the parking lot and ordered to sit down, next to Otieno, Jacob and Nahashon Juma who were also in custody. They were arresting the wrong group, with just one exception.

"You are making a mistake. The gunman is still in there!"

"Shut up!" Thwack. The constable guarding us almost cracked my head open with the butt of his gun.

Mburu looked at me and whispered that I needed to be quiet. I knew he was right.

The megaphone came on again as I looked around. The police had taken up positions, their guns trained on the door where the gunman was holed up. And Rosa! Had she made it out? I had to do something but my hands were tied - literally.

The door to the motel room opened a crack and I heard the clicks of police guns, hammers pulled back ready for action. I saw a hand waving and a woman's voice.

"Don't shoot, don't shoot!" It was Rosa - she stepped out, slowly, her hands raised above her head. A police officer walked towards her, gun ready, grabbed her and ran her off to safety.

"He is still in there with a gun!" she shouted as she was raced off harm's way.

"This is the last warning. Come out with your hands in the air. No one gets hurt, and we can all go home."

I saw the officer with the megaphone, a short man with thick legs, holster his pistol and pick up a shot gun.

They were going in.

About six officers lined up into an assault formation and headed towards the door. The leader gave some hand signals and they split up, three on either side of the door squatting - guns ready.

The short officer stood up and braced himself to the side of the door and then turned around and kicked it open and ran in sideways followed by his team.

We heard shouts: "Drop it! Drop it!"

Two thunderous shots rang out - unmistakably shotgun shells, followed by silence.

After a few tense seconds, the door opened slowly and the lead officer walked out followed by two officers, dragging a n wounded Kantar to the police van.

The short officer walked to where we were.

"Un-cuff them - except this one," he said pointing to Nahashon Juma. He then looked at me. "Jack Chidi...Detective Felix Dube with Internal Affairs," he introduced himself.

Just then, two officers walked out of the motel room dragging the gunman. They dropped his lifeless body on the pavement outside the door like a huge bean bag.

"Kamau Kariuk," I whispered to no one in particular, relieved that it had come to an end but not the way I had hoped. An arrest would have been fine. Felix Dube started to walk down to the body and I followed, slowly, to confirm what I already knew.

Felix knelt down and pulled the hood off. It was Detective Ali Fana!

Darkness.

CHAPTER TWENTY TWO

Several hours later, we were seated on a long leather chair in some office. Felix Dube sat across from us, behind a Mahogany desk. He was speaking to someone on the phone.

"What happened, man?" I asked Mburu who was sitting next to me.

"You passed out."

I looked around me and then it came back to me - Ali Fana, dead on a pavement.

Felix Dube was done on the phone. He pulled up a chair. In the office light, he was not really that short after all - stocky, yes.

"May I offer you gentlemen anything?"

"Perhaps an explanation," Otieno quipped. His grin was gone.

"As I told you, I am with Internal Affairs. Of course I know you, Jack Chidi and you, Otieno Kibogoye, of *The Daily Grind*, but I am not sure that I know you," he said, pointing at Jacob, "or the gun fighter," he added looking at Mburu.

"I run security for Wells Fargo," Mburu introduced himself.

Felix looked at Jacob as if to motion it was his turn.

"I'm a driver with *The Daily Grind*."

"Good. Now that we all know each other, we can begin. First off, let me say how sorry I am about your friend - I truly do not like taking out one of our own but he left me no choice in that matter - and thanks to you too, Mburu. He was wounded but he was not going to give himself up."

"I just don't understand how this whole operation connects…" I was still trying to process this mess.

"Off the record of course, I can tell you that I have never seen anything like it," Felix started. He leaned back on his chair and then cleared his throat.

He was about to explain when the phone rang. He stood up and walked behind his desk, picked it up and listened. Then he thanked the caller and walked back to where we were.

"We have Kamau Kariuki and his wife, Esther, in custody," he announced, smiling widely.

He pulled his seat and continued, "Yeah, where were we? Ah, yes! Oh, but before I forget, let me remind you that you will still have to record formal statements, you know, once we finish with this … er … unofficial chit-chat, eh?" He looked at me for confirmation. I nodded assent.

Felix Dube told us that he had been investigating Ali Fana and a cadre of officers for corruption for some time. This was after an internal audit was ordered by the new Police Commissioner who had been appointed to clean up the police department and restore public trust in law enforcement.

"Well, we suspected that Ali Fana might be dipping into some funny business after we learned that he and his wife, Fatima, had purchased two rental properties in Mombasa."

"What properties? They have the one house they just bought…"

I started to say but he did not let me finish.

"Believe me, they were in deep." His eyes lit up - focused and beady eyes.

"How do all these things translate to murder?" I asked.

He forced a chuckle and then looked at me and said, "In one word, – greed."

"How did they organise this operation?" Otieno asked, echoing my thoughts exactly.

"Well, Fatima, as a Real Estate agent was the one who identified potential house buyers, obviously wealthy men looking for property in and around Nairobi. Once identified, the victims were taken to KenView to see a model house as constructed by KayKay Concepts."

"But where does Ali Fana come in?" I asked impatiently.

"He is the law man - a rising star in the department, good detective. But he got in over his head when they entered the housing market - promises of great wealth. Now, you know KayKay Concepts actually started in Mombasa and when they went bankrupt - strapped for cash - Ali and Fatima bought those two properties from Kamau Kariuki just before his company went into receivership. Greed can do wonders. Ali Fana found himself with three mortgages and no cash to service them. He had to make some extra cash. So when he is approached by Kamau Kariuki with a housing scheme, he goes in, not knowing that it would escalate."

"So he was scammed into it?" I asked.

"Oh no! Not at all, you see, they were basically selling services that were not there. Ali was the legal arm, the protector, he was able to impede investigations, suppress evidence without which there would be no case. In fact, we are looking at all his arrests to make sure they were by the book and not just some cooked up charges to cover his tracks."

It was beginning to make sense, opening up a world of corruption and greed but my mind refused to accept that Rosa was part of it.

"And the Coroner?" I asked

"Bait!" He paused to look at me knowingly and then continued, "An easy thing for her to do, eh, Jack?"

"Yes, sir!" That I could see. "But why would she agree to murder? It's not like she needed money. She's a very highly accomplished person, brains and beauty, mind and body..." I caught myself becoming lyrical and emotional.

"Revenge can be a huge motivator, Mr. Chidi. You remember her father, Roberto? Remember how they hounded him like a criminal and then how he mysteriously died in a car accident? Well, perhaps to her all these rich bastards were to blame for his death."

"Are you talking about Roberto Alessandro - the Italian flower dude?" Otieno asked.

"Yes. That's Rosa's father. Why?" I asked.

"That was Ali's first high profile case straight from the academy!" Otieno boomed, eyes lighting up.

"That's right. Ali was preying on the misery of a grieving daughter whose father had been taken away from her, while she was using him to avenge his death," said Felix Dube.

"I have a question," Jacob said, a surprise because he and Mburu had stayed out of it for the most part.

"How come you seem to know a lot about us, I mean about Mr. Chidi here. Were you following us or something?"

"Okay, I will be very frank. As I said, we have been investigating your friend, Ali, for corruption for some time now but at first we did not know the depth of his involvement. There was no way we could really investigate his finances without alerting him except through following you, Chidi. In fact, we suspected you and Otieno were part of this gang. We had a tail on both of you."

"What? Since when?" I asked.

"Look, let's just say I was doing my job and we did not know where you fitted in. Surely, you cannot blame us for the company you keep. But when those two thugs attacked you," he said looking at me, "we knew that you were not involved. I'm surprised you did not recognise them from Limuru ... remember after Dr. Kizito?"

Ah, yes! The two guys who came in and started talking about Dr. Kizito ... the one with the lisp! Oh my god!

"You were following us even then?"

"Like I said, we have been at this for a while. But until those two thugs came at you, we had to treat you two as suspects."

"You were the one driving that car when I was attacked?"

"Yes. But you handled yourself so there was no need for us to intervene." He smiled but I did not see what he was smiling about. I did not see the humour. I was tired and despondent.

"Damn, man! What if they had shot me?" I asked.

He smiled enigmatically.

"Well, let me say upfront that you guys helped us a great deal, but

I would ask you to let professionals handle this type of thing in the future. Threatening suspects in their homes, gunfights in the middle of the road - jeez, I really had to ignore quite a lot of complaints against you, guys. But all is well that ends well, I suppose. Shall we record your statements?"

"Oh, one more thing: Wagateru - how does he fit in?" I asked.

"Wagateru was taken out by Nahashon - no lose ends - what we call collateral damage."

Timorously, I asked him about Meredith.

"Who is Meredith?" He looked around, puzzled. I explained.

"Hmm, we did not have anything on her at all. But we will investigate."

Felix Dube stood up and went to his desk. He retrieved a piece of paper and reading from it he offered us the official version of events.

I fully understood.

Before we left, I asked Otieno, Mburu and Jacob to wait for me in the car. I had one favour to ask of Felix.

"It's okay, Mr. Chidi, you can let them go, and I will drive you to your office."

"That's okay with us, Jack," Otieno said and they walked out.

I turned to Felix. I think he knew what I wanted to talk about. He asked me to take a walk with him even before I had uttered a word.

As we walked down a long corridor, I asked him about Fatima. He did not respond at once, and I assumed that she had met the same fate as her husband - Jesus, the kids!

"Well, between you and me, we know that she was fucking that scumbag, and that she spotted the victims. But I think we have seen enough pain and suffering." He walked on. I did not ask for him to elaborate.

At the end of the hallway, we stopped at a holding cell. He pointed at the door and I peeked in through the small glass window. Rosa was sitting with her head buried in her knees. Felix rapped on the door and then pulled out a key and opened it. She looked up and saw me.

Our eyes met and held for a brief instant before hers fell. I felt sorry for her - it was a different kind of sorry. I started to say something but words failed me and I did not say whatever I had wanted to say or ask. I had turned to walk away when I heard her whisper my name and I turned round.

"Thank you," she said and her eyes came up to mine.

"For what?" I asked in astonishment.

She paused for a minute as if looking for the right word.

"For forgiveness - remember what you said about forgiveness the other night?"

"Ah, yes, but you want me to forgive you?" I asked almost angrily.

"No, you somehow challenged me to learn to forgive so that I could live. This was going to be my last one. Please believe me."

She looked different. But I did not understand what she meant and I was going to press her to elaborate but decided against it. What did it matter now?

CHAPTER TWENTY THREE

● ● ● · ● ● ●

We worked feverishly to get the story out the next day on a special edition of *The Daily Grind*. It was the hardest piece I have ever worked on. Ali, in a strange and twisted way, had kept his promise of giving me headlines.

Bulldog was elated that we had the story but he reminded me to remain objective. I guess he was right, this time, given my close association to Ali, my emotional attachment to Rosa and the missing Meredith. It was sad to know that someone so close to me could commit such atrocities. I tried to detach myself from the betrayal, the fear, the deception and loss but it was like taking the white out of milk.

No one could have foreseen it but the death of Isaac King'ori would affect my life in very profound ways. I did not personally know the man but his life, or the end of it, would take me into the bowels of evil.

My mother had told me once that the devil's dwelling was always within arm's length and that if you looked hard enough you could smell it. I had never given it much thought until I was knee deep in the bog.

If truth be told, I had also learned a little bit about myself from wading through the morass of corruption and greed. My baptism of fire, I called it.

They say that what does not kill you makes you stronger and wiser. There is some truth in that. However, they fail to mention that it also leaves you scarred, skeptical and afraid. I took heart in knowing that time would allow the wounds to heal but I knew that something deep down inside me would always remain raw, tender and torn.

I had called Ben three times to inquire about Meredith but he had not heard from her. Felix Dube had nothing on her and there had been no reports of unidentified bodies at the mortuaries. It seemed she had simply disappeared into thin air. But how could it be? I resigned to just waiting and hoping that I would not get that one phone call that we all dreaded.

Thursday morning, two days after the story broke out, I decided to walk to Uhuru Park. Well, I had two reasons. One, I wanted to place a flower by the entrance where Wagateru had been found, and two, I wanted to get away from the office and decide how to go about looking for Meredith, dead or alive. I had to find her - I did not think I should just sit and hope.

By the pond, watching the ducks bathe, I remembered how pretentious I thought ducks were and I smiled. I was right though, they had an easy, unencumbered manner about them - not a care in the world.

I opened the paper I had with me and turned to the sports section. Manchester United's loss to Arsenal had ignited riots in London that had continued for days. There was a picture of a policeman with a Billy-club raised to the buttocks of a rioter, who, with pants sagging at the hips, was having a hard time escaping, which reminded me of Otieno and his wife.

My phone rang. I answered it, as I had done so many times, with trepidation.

It was Meredith. I jumped up from the bench.

"What happened - where are you?" I asked, telling her that I had called for her at the Grill and spoken to Ben.

"Yeah, he told me." She sounded good.

"What happened? Are you okay? You just disappeared."

"Well, the two men who came to see me demanded that I make you stop; that they would hurt me if I did not. At the time, I did not know what they were talking about and I knew that there was no way I could ask you to stop hunting for the killer. So I went into hiding. I was at Ben's all this time."

That damn rascal! I smiled, knowing that he had done the right thing.

"Jack, I'm sorry about your friend. I know what it's like to be betrayed."

We arranged to meet for lunch, finally.

On my way back to the office, my phone rang. It was Bulldog.

"Hello?" I graveled.

"How soon can you get back?"

I knew it before I answered that this could only mean one thing but he did not let me answer.

It was an order, not a request.

Printed in the United States
By Bookmasters